Zugzwang

By

Nicola Fisher

To Max

My office buddy

Chapter 1

The darkness was increasing. September. The night rolled down the hills settling on the houses, shops, and offices of the town beneath. It was Thursday. Almost the end of the working week for most; they were buzzing around finishing off the last tasks. Depositing letters to the post room to be sent out in the morning, leaving post-it notes on their desks to remind them of the things they couldn't be bothered to finish off on Thursday and needed to be done by the end of the week. Many had already left and were gathering supplies for the weekend, wine, beer, ready meals, giant bags of crisps, then struggling with an unruly shopping trolley through the grimy yellow light of a supermarket car park.

One of these people was Jenna Bishop. She finished work at 5pm promptly. She zipped up her jacket and headed out across the car park. She was not permitted to park in the car park outside of her office, you needed a permit for that and Jenna was number 144 on the waiting list. She parked across the road on the shopping complex with the other also-rans. Tonight, she had to walk past her car on to the supermarket. As she marched through the increasingly cold air she reiterated her shopping list in her head – toothpaste, her mum never bought the one that Jenna liked, she liked the one that made your teeth whiter - a pizza, a giant bag of crisps and a bottle of wine. She grabbed a shopping trolley and began to wonder around the supermarket. Once she got home she would run a bath, light some scented candles, but a face pack on, a deep conditioner on her hair, then she would apply her fake tan, ready for Friday night. She had her outfit sorted already. She ordered online earlier in the week but she had to get it delivered to work as her mum was on at about her spending. She kept telling her she should be putting money aside for a deposit on her own house. That could wait. Jenna was quite happy living at home for the time being, it meant she had more money to spend on nights out with her friends and new clothes. There would be plenty of time for responsibility. She would only be young once.

Jenna went back to planning her evening. When she was done with her beauty prep, she would put on her favourite pyjamas, put her pizza in the oven, pour a glass of wine and snuggle down on the sofa for the night with a DVD. Bliss. Now with the shopping trolley full and her car insight she was almost there.

She loaded the bags into the boot of the car closed it and climbed in to the driver's side. It was starting to get dark, the street light above her car was broken. The car's sunroof leaked and the windscreen and rear mirror constantly misted up. Jenna hurriedly began to wipe them, she wanted to get home. She wiped the windscreen first, then the rear-view mirror. She stopped. Her eyes were fixed on the rear-view mirror, she did not turn around. Staring back at her was a pair of deep dark eyes that belonged to the hooded figure on the back seat. Jenna looked deep in to the eyes. She wanted to run, she wanted to scream, but she was frozen. Unable to move, unable to make a sound, terror seized her. A gloved hand wrapped around her neck.

Chapter 2

The alarm was like a drill. It buried deep into Oscar's head and forced him to open his eyes and hit the snooze button. Ten more minutes, he thought. Ten minutes goes pretty quickly when it's early and soon the drill started again. He heaved himself in to a sitting position placed his feet on the floor. "Three" he said out loud. It was Tuesday feet on the floor and out of bed meant he was up and there were only three early get ups to go until weekend. Then he could lie in bed as long as he wanted. Maybe even all day, that had become a bit of a habit lately. Last Saturday it had got light then gone dark again before he surfaced and that was only because hunger had overcome his desire to just lie there. Opening the door to takeaway delivery drivers was the about the only contact he had with people outside work these days.

He picked his dressing gown up off the floor and wrapped it around him. The house was cold, he really needed to start setting the timer on the central heating but he never quite sussed how to get it right. That has always been Marie's job.

He shuffled across the landing to the bathroom and turned on the shower. He yawned into the mirror as the room filled with steam. He looked tired, he thought, he was sure it hadn't always been this way. There had been a time when he would put off going to sleep for as long as possible too busy working, thinking. Many times, he didn't make it to bed at all but would fall asleep at his desk then wake up after only a few hours ready to go again. Nothing faded him. But not anymore, he had faded in every way. It showed in the mirror and in the way, he felt every morning when the alarm sounded.

The shower was meant to revive him, it wasn't working. He stood under the hot water and let it run over him. Six more months, he thought, just six more months then he would be retired. Being a police officer was the only job he had ever done, the only job he had ever wanted to do. He had progressed through the ranks to become Detective Superintendent something his teenage self would have been delighted with.

He grabbed the shower dial and turned it all the way round to cold. He screamed and jumped backwards nearly losing his balance as the blast of cold water hit him in the face. Then he grabbed the dial again and turned the shower off. It had helped, a little.

He wandered back across the landing to his bedroom and began getting dressed. He could not remember the last time he had worn a piece of clothing that had been ironed. After doing up the buttons on his shirt he attempted to fasten his tie, the red silk between his fingers was smooth and cold. He remembered feeling it as he ripped open the wrapping paper, why do people buy men ties as presents? he'd thought, men have ties anyway. Still he smiled and said thank you. Marie has smiled back, "just your colour" she'd said. Pleased she'd made the right choice. Oscar looked down at the tangled mess in his hands today and threw it to one side. He would go without tie, again. He ran a hair brush through his hair now filled with grey but still thick, at least he'd managed to cling on to something he thought.

He made his way downstairs in his crumpled suit, the creak of each stair seemed loud in the big empty house. In the hallway there was a heap of junk mail that he had allowed to pile up. There was a library of takeaway menus, adverts for driveway paving and leaflets letting him know that where there's blame there's a claim. Oscar told himself that when he retired he would use his days to tidy the house, iron his clothes, and cook proper meals but he already knew it was a lie. His heart had always been in the job, top detective on the force, best arrest record in the country. When he got a sniff of a lead he did not let it go. He was blinkered to the rest of reality; the case and solving it occupied his every thought. Nothing else had mattered.

He moved around the house in autopilot; he found his car keys where he'd dumped them on the stairs when he came home the previous evening. Then he went in to the living room to try and find his shoes; he jumped back when he put his foot on chess piece that was on the floor in the living room. He picked it up – Why was it there? ... Oh yes, he had been playing online chess with Ivan from Kentucky until three in the morning, now the chess pieces were scattered across the living room. Ivan had won. Chess was another area where Oscar felt himself fading. It was game he'd always been good at. He enjoyed the strategy, trying to suss out his opponents next move. But lately his concentration had waned, Ivan had beaten him the last three games in a row.

Oscar found his shoes and out them on. He looked at his watch, late again; he would just have to get a coffee when he got to work. He grabbed the plastic lunch box from the fridge in the kitchen. He had a least bothered to make himself a packed lunch last night. It was something Marie had always insisted on, she felt that buying sandwiches was a waste of money. He picked up his wallet and phone and headed out the door. He didn't bother with a jacket, although as he shut the door behind him he started to regret his decision. The clouds above were thick and beginning to darken. A gust of wind blew some of the leaves that had already started to fall. Oscar stopped at the car door unsure if he'd heard a rumble of thunder. He stood still and listened, it seemed quiet for now. He opened the car door and got inside.

Oscar's house was perched high on the side of a hill. From the back garden you could see over the town in the valley below. He reversed his car out of his drive way and drove down the road that snaked its way past the other houses and down in to the town. Hoddlesworth was a fairly ordinary town. It nestled in the foothills of the Pennines which meant the weather was damp most of the time. It had once been a home to miners and mill workers. Hardworking people grafting in dirt and sweat. These days Hoddlesworth stood at the ends of grasping fingers of the other northwest cities, where rural life rolled in to industry and back again. Like many towns it was divided in to two halves. On one side there was a mix of large new polished houses, renovated stylish cottages and barn conversions. Here were the executives who commuted to the cities frequenting the train station and motorway junction, but preferred lush green views at home.

The other half of the town was made up of 1960s houses, tower blocks, and of rows of Victorian terraced houses once home to the miners and mill workers; many were now boarded up or in a bad state of repair as the generations who were left after the mines and mills closed struggled with unemployment.

There was still a weekly market in the town centre although its size had dwindled over the years. Once the bustling heart of the town it now consisted of a butcher's van and a couple who sold clothing seconds. Surrounding the market square were a number of shops that used to be occupied by greengrocers, butchers, a bakery even a wool shop and haberdashery. They had all now closed. There were a few cafés left but most of the other units had been changed to nail parlours, charity shops, takeaways and estate agents. There was a small budget supermarket but most people did their shopping at large modern out of town supermarkets and shopping centres.

Oscar had grown up here in one of the old Victorian terraces. He had known this place when it still had a soul; it had known him when he still had a soul. Now each morning as he drove to work, he felt with certainty, that they were both getting closer and closer to giving up.

Chapter 3

James Miller downed his espresso. He placed his cup on the kitchen counter then tapped his coffee making machine as if to say another job well done. It was early morning and he needed the assistance. His coffee maker was his pride and joy. He had treated himself to it last February. It was expensive, top of the range, the best. He had debated with himself about whether or not to buy it for a while. He visited the coffee maker on numerous shopping trips and he could feel the weight of his father's disapproval every time he checked the price tag.

It was, in the end, this disapproval that convinced him to eventually buy the coffee maker. He had gone around to his parent's house for Sunday dinner; it was February, close to Valentine's Day. His mother did her usual not so subtle probing in to his love life, by asking him if he had any gifts to buy. When he said that he hadn't and joked that he just waited for the gifts to come to him he felt his father's disapproving stare floating to him over the gravy. When he got home that evening he decided to buy himself a gift, the coffee maker.

James picked up his car keys and an organic protein bar from the kitchen counter and headed for the door. He opened the door to his car. It was a BMW 4 series convertible, his second favourite possession, after the coffee maker. The car purred in to life. He had chosen it in white and was very particular about keeping it clean, so it looked like the paint work glowed. His father said it made him look like a drug dealer, but James liked it. James ripped open the protein bar with his teeth and one hand, the other hand working the steering wheel.

He turned on to the main street and clicked on the radio. It had just hit the hour and the jingle for the news bulletin sounded. James listened closely; there was a political rant about immigration, a story about fracking protests, and a story about an actor building an eco-home, then it switched to sporting updates.

The next song came on the radio and he sang along. The sun was just starting to rise and it cast and orange glow on the fog that had descended overnight. James wasn't far away from the station when his phone rang. He pressed the button on the hands free when he saw Evelyn's name.

"We've got one" she said straight away. James' hands tightened on the wheel.

"Well good morning to you DI Patterson" James said.

"Good morning sir." Evelyn replied "But we've got one." Evelyn seemed calm and in control. A bit of a cold fish he thought at first but she was good at her job.

"Ok, fill me in on scene I'll make my way there now. What's the location?"

Evelyn provided the details "Boss?" she said "This is weird."

"Ok. Be with you in ten."

James disconnected the call and changed lanes. The traffic lights turned red. He let out a deep breath, adjusted his tie then touched his forehead to check for any signs of perspiration. They had one. He had been made head of the murder investigation team three months ago but so far all he'd were open and shut cases domestics, drug dealers settling debts. No real cases, nothing where he could really show his skills. Until now.

The filter light turned green and James turned the corner and carried on to the crime scene.

He pulled into the car park; he saw the white tent and parked not too far from it. James sat behind the steering wheel of his car staring ahead but in his vision was only fog. Was he up to this? It was what he'd always wanted but now the moment was here he wasn't sure. He knew that fairly soon he would have to open the door, step outside with his usual air of confidence and give the other officers some answers. He was one of the youngest officers ever to make DCI. His colleagues either worshiped him or they hated him and James loved it. His name was known. His smile, his swagger came naturally, he didn't have to put on a show. He had always been confident, arrogant some might say. Failure was not something James was used to.

There was a tap at the window. He didn't need to look who it was he adjusted his collar and opened the door. "Good morning DI Patterson, what do we have?" James said.

"I was starting to thing you weren't going to join us DCI Miller?" Evelyn Patterson said.

"Just waiting to make my grand entrance"

"Hmmm. This way."

The two of them walked across the car park to the police cordon. Evelyn had only recently been assigned to James' department. He didn't know a lot about her, he had not made much effort to find out. He had heard she was an academic, a criminologist turned copper. James wasn't keen on criminologists, thought the answers to solving crimes could be found in books or computer programmes. Evelyn was tall, she walked purposefully. Even thought her body looked strong her facial features were delicate and fragile. The eyelashes that framed her grey-green eyes were so fair they were almost in visible and she never put make up on them. Her mousey brown hair that James suspected had been blonde as a child had darkened with age but she had not decided to dye it, perhaps for fear of vanity.

Evelyn gestured towards the white SOCO tent "The victim. Female early twenties…"

"Early twenties?" James interrupted

"Yes" Evelyn continued, "Female early twenties. Found by a parking attendant early this morning. Initial assessment would indicate the cause of death was strangulation. No signs of forced entry or damage to the vehicle. She's still in the driver's seat, fully clothed. Her hair's been cut off. Hacked at, it would seem and it looks like was wearing makeup that's been wiped off and smudged over her face."

James stared into the middle distance. He hoped he looked assured but his mind was whirling desperately trying to find an answer. Early twenties? She would have had plans for the future, a family would miss her, parents who would never have thought they'd have to go through this. James felt the weight of the responsibility growing on him and suddenly this didn't feel so exciting.

"This, cutting her hair wiping her makeup off it seems personal, like it was done in anger. "Evelyn said "My guess is this is an open and shut crime of passion. Ex-boyfriend, rejected suitor, perhaps."

A SOCO emerged from the white tent "Sir! Sir we found something you might need to take a look at?" the SOCO shouted.

James and Evelyn marched over "What is it?" James asked.

The SOCO held up a small scrap of paper and unravelled it carefully so as not to contaminate any evidence "It was in the victim's throat. It looks like a web address."

Just then Evelyn was sick on the tarmac and excused herself. James went inside the tent. The victim was still sitting in the driver's seat of her car. Her dark hair had been cut, down to a couple of inches, the remains of it were scattered over her clothing and around the car, make-up smudged across her face like someone had scrubbed at it. Something sparkled on the victim's lap and caught James' eye, he put on pair of gloves and picked it up. It was an earring, silver with a purple tear drop stone in the middle. He moved the victims head and looked at her ears, there was no other earring. James handed the earring to the SOCO, "Bag this up" he said "And check everywhere, there should be two of these. If one is missing I need to know about it."

Chapter 4

The police station was on the opposite side of the town to where Oscar lived. A dirty beige 1960s building that clung to the edge of the town at the point where it dissipated back in to moorland.

Oscar sat and stared at the computer screen. The rest of the office buzzed around him; ants holding up blades of grass to prove their worth. His eyes deviated occasionally to the world beyond his glass bubble. He used to be like them once; enthusiastic, eager to please, staying late, working through lunch breaks, pulling all nighters. It all mattered so much; he thought he could change the world. Keep the baddies off the streets; give the good guys the justice they deserved. His fight, his vigour had seen him rise to the top. The ants out there now looked up to him. If they had enough fight enough vigour, if they pull enough all nighters, work through enough lunch breaks, work enough weekends one day they could be sitting in his chair.

Oscar put his hand on the arm of the chair and felt the discoloured sponge bursting through the threadbare upholstery. He turned his attention back to the screen and debated whether to put the eight on the nine of diamonds or to deal again. He'd only been there an hour and already he was fed up. Six more months, he reminded himself, but then what? Oscar was the job it had possessed every corner of his being, he had forgotten everything else around him. Now there was nothing else around him. As much as he didn't want to be there anymore he didn't know where else to be. He moved his eyes away from the computer screen and stared out of the window at the bleak expansive moorland.

Finally, it came around to lunch time. Oscar shuffled in to the lunch room and filled the kettle with water and then he dumped a tea bag in to his favourite mug. It was chipped and stained brown on the inside from many years of tea brewing, another thing Marie would scold him for "you should brew tea in a tea pot" she would say, and he would insist he didn't have time. It was Marie who had bought him the mug; Oscar had been in his study going over case notes, he got angry with her for insisting he stop working and come down to dinner. He woke up slumped over the case notes on his desk the next morning Marie had already left for her job at the library. When he came down the mug was on the kitchen counter "Mr Grumpy" it said. There was a note next to stating Marie had bought the mug for his birthday but decided the occasion had warranted giving it to him early. She was always so patient, so understanding. If only he's appreciated it at the time.

The kettle bubbled and clicked bringing Oscar back to reality. He yawned and poured the hot water over the tea bag. It was quiet in the lunch room, he liked to get in there early before the rush. The actual canteen had been done away with a while ago. It had been the social hub of the station serving real hot food, cooked on site, by real people. But the real people cost too much and the space was deemed more valuable as extra offices so now they had The Lunch Room. It was a dismal room with windows down one wall that overlooked the car park, a table and a couple of chairs, a fridge, a kettle and a microwave. There was a bin the corner which overflowed with rubbish and always seemed to be few dirty pots in the sink. Oscar thought it was a ploy to stop people lingering too long and take their lunch back to their desks to eat so they would keep working.

A few other people filtered in playing with their phones and stirring things in Tupperware containers. Oscar opened the fridge and took out his little plastic lunch box in which were the ham sandwiches he had lazily prepared for himself; processed cheap ham, basic cheap white bread. Marie liked to cook. Lasagne was her speciality; he could still remember that garlicky cheesy smell when he walked through the door at the end of a long day. They had spent a wonderful holiday in Italy. They travelled by train visiting Rome, Florence, Venice and Naples; warm summer evenings wandering through narrow cobbled streets. He remembered one night in particular they had a long day sightseeing in Florence. His feet ached and his stomach rumbled. They had wondered down a small back street and spotted a little café with small metal tables and chairs outside under a colourful canopy. They sat down as an enthusiastic waiter came over to greet them. They ordered drink red wine and a pasta dish neither of them could pronounce but it was smothered in a delicious rich tomato sauce with garlic, herbs and cheese. Oscar remembered on that night the job had felt so far away it was just him and Marie and at that moment that was all that had mattered to him. He had looked up at the indigo sky and smiled.

He found a seat in the lunch room, scraping the chair leg across the lino floor and he sat down. The brown plastic table top was sticky, there were coffee cup rim marks and the remains of salads, sandwiches, and crisps, scattered across the surface. He stood up, got some paper towels and wiped it down.

"Cuts hitting us that badly Gov?" a voice said. Oscar looked up and saw Arthur Doyle a DI who had been based in Hoddlesworth nearly as long as Oscar had. He had been DI for a long time and never expressed any desire to climb further. He wore a brown suit with a kind of grey shirt that Oscar assumed must have once been white and was now half tucked in to his too-tight trousers. His tie left a gap between his unfastened top shirt buttons but the knot was pulled too tight as if it was never undone just loosened and tightened again every night and every morning. "Things must be bad when the Detective Superintendent has to start moonlighting as a cleaner," Arthur laughed loudly and to himself. He put his hands in his pockets and leaned back as though he was proud of his comedic exploits. Oscar attempted a smile to humour him but he suspected his contempt was obvious.

"Someone left this table in a right state. Clearly not very house proud." Oscar thought about the state of his own kitchen at home, what would people think of him if they saw that?

"Ah animals some of these lot sir, dread to think what their own houses must look like" Oscar raised his eyebrow and nodded "Anyway I best get back to it. No rest for the wicked eh?" He laughed again "Or should I say the wicked never rest?" he laughed louder. Oscar remained expressionless. "I'll leave you to it, do you want this paper?" He took a copy of the local paper from under his arm and placed in on the table before Oscar had a chance to answer his question "See you later Gov" Arthur called over his shoulder as he left.

Oscar was relieved; he hated people wanting to sit with him at lunch. His previous excuse had been he was surrounded by people all day firing questions at him, expecting answers. These days though it was mostly just him by himself all day long in his little office trawling through a pile of paper work. Hardly anyone came in to speak to him anymore. Jean, his PA, well, the teams PA as she was these days, would pop in at regular intervals and ask if he wanted coffee. There was a time when she would chat to him, ask him how he was doing, tell him about her life; about how her grandson was doing at university, how proud she was of him. Had he graduated now? Oscar realised he had no idea; it must have been some time since Jean had felt the need to chat with him. The only other times he interacted with people were in the boring budget meetings he was forced to sit through once a month. He usually tried to get out of them but The Chief would contact him directly. His absences had not gone unnoticed, she had told him, and then she proceeded to remind him of the importance of budget targets, MI reports, and spread sheets. She would continue with a well-rehearsed spiel about how they were a proactive force and that meant they needed to meet targets in all areas, not just arrest statistics but budgets too. Oscar had nodded off in one particularly long and tedious meeting, The Chief had not been happy with that. He had been summoned to her office to explain himself like a naughty school boy caught playing truant. He had been working very hard, he told her, long hours, lots of over time – unpaid of course- he had not been getting much sleep. He had not been falling back in to bad habits had he? She enquired; Oscar answered confirming he had not.

As a result of his napping The Chief now contacted him directly before every meeting to make sure he was alert and ready. He would assure her that he was but deep down he couldn't care less about the stupid meeting. He didn't really care what The Chief thought about him anymore either. What could she do to him now? He would be retired in six months.

He took the last mechanical bite of his sandwich, screwed up the tin foil it had been wrapped in and put it in the bin. Oscar glanced over at the paper Arthur had left on the table and something caught his eye. The front page was mostly taken up by an advert for a carpet shop rather than a major scoop. Free papers had to make their money somehow, he supposed. Underneath though there was a news story and a name he recognised. He didn't want to look at it but his curiosity got the better of him. Oscar unfolded the paper and saw the full headline "20th Anniversary appeal for Worthington Farm Massacre" He continued reading "Today marks the 20th anniversary of the Worthington Farm Massacre. Mr and Mrs Worthington and their three sons Jack three, Stephen six and Thomas eight, were all found murdered in their home 20 years ago today. The bodies were discovered by their eldest daughter Carrie Worthington, 15, who was still at school at the time of the attack and the only surviving member of the family. Despite the brutal nature of this attack no suspect has ever been charged. If anyone remembers anything about that day of has any further information please contact us." There was a small box at the bottom of the page containing a phone number and an email address. Oscar felt his throat go dry. He took a sip of his tea but it didn't quite cut it and he poured it down the sink.

Chapter 5

The place was small, grim. The peeling red and white sign stuck to the window said "Café" but Hoddlesworth was certainly a town yet to embrace European café culture. It didn't really have the weather for it. Outside the fog was lifting but there was no hope of any breaks of sunlight, just dismal darkness stretching out across the town and across the hills beyond.

James sat down and made sure he was facing the widow, he liked to keep an eye on what was happening. Nothing would get past him. He would be vigilant. Evelyn sat opposite him; she still looked pale and stayed silent. The waitress came over to take their order, she had tried to pin her greyish/brownish/reddish greasy hair up, in a vain attempt to comply with health and safety regulations, however she failed miserably as bits of it broke free and clung to her puffed up face. She wiped her hands on her apron then took a small note pad and a well chewed pencil out of the pocket and stood waiting for them to give her their order; she did not bother to speak or make eye contact.

"Two black coffees please "James said.

"You sure you don't want anything to eat?" James asked Evelyn "It seemed you lost most of your breakfast back there?"

"I'm fine" Evelyn replied abruptly, shaking her head and straightening her jacket. The waitress grunted in acknowledgment and walked away.

"I puked on my first" James said "Smack head. Battered to death for not paying up to a dealer. The guy had been lying dead in his bedsit for a fortnight before anyone noticed the smell." He swallowed hard as the memory came back to him. Evelyn gave tight smile and nodded before turning her attention back to her lapels.

The waitress returned with the coffees and put them down on the table. James picked up his cup and took a sip. Evelyn tentatively touched her finger tips against the warmth of the coffee cup, her eyes fixed on the swirling bubbles. "It's not my first," she said allowing her eyes to drift around the café then fixing them back on James, "I've been on the force for ten years now. Before that I lectured in Criminal Psychology, so I've heard plenty of gruesome tales but this one just made me so angry." She paused and her fingers gripped the handle of the cup making her knuckles turn white "she was just so young" she let out a long breath and realised her grip slightly "I mean, the way that girl died was written all over her face. She died terrified and alone." Evelyn sipped at her coffee "It's one thing reading things in books, but their faces, do their faces ever leave you?"

James took a sip of his coffee and placed the cup back down on the table "Not completely, if you want the truth. But I don't think that they should. If you can wipe them away, box them up with the mundane then you've stopped caring. You can learn to control their access though, banish them when you need to focus on something else. When they do get through it reminds you that you still care, that you still have a passion." He thought of one face in particular, the one that made sure he never lost his passion, not again.

"And you need passion to catch the bad guys"

"Indeed, you do" James smiled and leaned back in his chair. "So, was it a passion to catch the bad guys that made you want to join the police?"

"It was. I like to keep challenging myself. After my divorce I decided a change of direction was in order. I guess I wanted to make a difference. Go to bed at the end of the day feeling like I've done something, something that matters. Not just clocking in and going through the motions until it's time to go home again but actually having an impact in someone's life, and maybe I like to surprise people, challenge their expectations." She smiled and took another sip of coffee.

James smiled back. "You know I'm not exactly a veteran at this game, but I've seen a lot of people coming into this job because they get off on throwing their weight around, intimidating people, boosting their ego. You have had some people telling you I'm one of them, but that's not what I'm about."

"Isn't it?"

"No. It's like you said, it's about going to bed and feeling like you've done something worthwhile. So, when the faces do come to get you, and they usually come at night, you still sleep soundly because you know you did everything you could." James downed his coffee and shuffled in his seat. "Anyway, time to get back to it."

They gathered their coats, James took a ten-pound note from his pocket and tossed it on to the table, knowing it was generous for two black coffees and making sure Evelyn saw it. He ushered Evelyn out of the door before the waitress had a chance to give him any change.

Outside the grey skies had dissipated to drizzle "Are you ok to make your way back to the station?" James asked.

"Yes, I've got my car," she said.

Chapter 6

Evelyn sat in the driver's seat of her car and took a deep breath. She felt better after that black coffee; steadier. She looked at herself in the rear-view mirror and was angry. She looked flustered, messy, amateur. She took a small hairbrush out of her bag and ran it through her hair then smoothed it down with her fingers. She took out a powder compact and dabbed her face then smoothed a little transparent balm across her lips. She liked to create the illusion that she wasn't wearing any make-up, that she was naturally perfect, flawless. It took her a lot of time and effort to perfect that look.

She was angry with herself just throwing up on the car park like some kid on work experience. What must he have thought of her? The way he spoke to her in the café; she could tell he thought she couldn't hack it, just another stupid woman who couldn't stand the sight of blood or the smell of a dead body. That had never bothered her at all; in fact, she found it fascinating. She remembered as a young child being fascinated by a cat that had been run over by a car. Its body was still in the road but the head had been detached. She knew the cat it used to sit on the fence post and hiss at anyone who passed, even the dogs. She saw it fight with a big dog once and the dog came off worse. It didn't seem right somehow to see it broken so easily.

Evelyn thought it was interesting to see the links that had held it together. Her mother went nuts when she saw it, she started screaming and crying then threw up like Evelyn had today. Then she called the council and demanded the cat be removed. It amazed Evelyn how life could be so fragile, everything at the mercy of the weakness of the physical body, however strong the spirit might be.

Evelyn punched the steering wheel. James was going to think she was pathetic now. She had always thought her mother was pathetic when she threw up at the sight of the cat that day, now she would be seen as the same. But it wasn't fear or disgust that made her sick, it was anger. That girl was just too young, it didn't seem fair.

It was the death of the cat that led Evelyn to study criminology. She found it interesting what went on inside the mind of a person who thought it was ok to take someone else's life. She had immersed herself in her studies. It wasn't difficult, she loved it; it was far more interesting than anything that happened on a night out with her housemates or anything that was on TV. This was real. It was her enthusiasm that had first made Brian notice her. She asked so many questions and she would stay behind after lectures and he would talk to her. She would go to his office and he would give her essay tips, then they met in the pub, then at his place. They had to be careful though, he said. Although they weren't doing anything illegal it could be seen as unprofessional and jeopardise his position.

They moved in together after she graduated, everybody had already known about them. She knew there was gossip but she didn't care. In fact, she quite liked it, thinking that people were talking about them. She carried on studying post grad and eventually became a lecturer herself, but somehow it always seemed flat. Talking about things she'd read in books wasn't enough she wanted to see it for real, see a real crime scene and look in to the eyes of a real criminal. That was when she decided to join the police force. Brian didn't like it but she was past caring about what he thought by then. She felt she had more than outgrown him, she had surpassed him. When she was student she looked up to

Brian, she felt blessed by the knowledge he bestowed on her, but it got to the point where the roles were reversed and she didn't feel there was anything left for her in the relationship. Her work was everything.

She drove to the station and parked the car. She had been angry at the way James spoke to her though he seemed to be like that with everyone. She had heard people talking around the station. He wasn't as popular as he thought he was, a lot of people thought him arrogant, that he had ideas about his station. James had only been working there two months longer than Evelyn had; she had been assigned to that department a month ago. He had barely spoken to her about anything other than work. She quite admired him for that. He had focus but so did she, she just wished he would let her show it.

Chapter 7

Lucy Maxwell shivered. She leaned back against the concrete wall and looked down the alleyway in front of her. It was evening in summer, still daylight. The shadows from the tower blocks now cast long across the tarmac. Kids were still playing out in the street wearing shorts and t-shirts, kicking footballs, shouting, and laughing. Lucy still felt cold. She pulled her coat around her tighter; the fake fur was matted and dirty. People passing gave her strange looks. How could she wear a coat like that in this weather? She remembered the day she found that coat; it was in a vintage shop in Chester. She'd spent the day wondering around the town with her flatmate Katie. Their flat was freezing as they never had enough money to top up the electricity card. Lucy had met Katie at university where they were studying art and design but they'd both dropped out of their courses with a plan to start a handmade jewellery business. That hadn't really worked out. They'd reverted to bar work and waitressing in the evenings and spent their days wondering around the city. It didn't seem to matter that they didn't have much money though they always seemed to manage to have a good time. As soon as Lucy saw the coat she had to have it. It was light grey with small flecks of black and made her feel like a 1940s film star. And it was warm.

Today Lucy felt cold all over, the little hairs on her body stood to attention as her skin goose pimpled. Sweat began seeping through her hair and down her face. She reached to wipe it away quickly, her face felt cold and clammy like a raw chicken. She remembered putting her makeup on for one of her many nights out with Katie, drinking cheap wine together while they got themselves ready. Bar work and waitressing wasn't really making ends meet though and they got deeper into the winter they constantly cold flat and constantly empty cupboards was starting to get them both down. The nights out were becoming fewer too as they never had enough money. Katie had met a new boyfriend Lucy had only met him a couple of times and she wasn't keen on him. There was something creepy out him. Katie told her he'd had an idea of how they could make more money. That is would be easy money.

Lucy's eyes surveyed the other people in the street, the kids playing, mums pushing prams. A jogger went past her, could they see? Could they see her drenched in clammy sweat? They didn't seem to pay her any attention if they did see. Maybe they were just going to let her drown in it? That was it, they were just going to carry on with their day while she stood there drowning right in front of them. Choking, coughing, clambering to the surface trying to break free and take a breath just to be pulled back down again splattering and pleading. They would all just carry on playing football and pushing prams and jogging and leave her to drown.

Lucy felt her breathing getting faster. He was late. What if he didn't turn up like the last time? What would she do then? If he just left her there shivering, gasping for air until she was a drowned and frozen body on the pavement. Last time he said he had been held up. It was unavoidable, he'd said, he couldn't get away. She had heard talk that the police had taken him away for questioning but he had been released without charge. Lucy was sure he just kept her waiting on purpose just to mess with her. That's what he was doing now, messing with her. With each second that passed she felt surer of it. Her hand tightened around the flick knife in her pocket, she always kept it with her for protection. It came in handy for punters who thought it was ok to leave without paying.

It had always been just alcohol, too much sometimes. But when she started waiting for Katie's boyfriend somehow it wasn't enough. He always had something to hand, something to make it all go away.

"Lucy, how's my favourite girl doing today?" he stood in the archway at the end of the alleyway the sunlight glinting off his leather jacket and shaved head. He walked down the alleyway towards her and the darkness wrapped around him.

"You're late" she said.

He stopped and glanced at his watch theatrically, "Actually my angel I think you'll find I'm early." He turned his wrist towards her and thrust it forward quickly so the watch was just a few inches from her face. Lucy leaned back instinctively and hit her head on the wall behind, he laughed. She squinted, her vision blurry and her head confused. She couldn't make out the time and she couldn't be bothered to argue with him, she just wanted what she came for.

"You want to get yourself a decent watch my dear, comes in handy. Maybe you should think about upping your prices a little." He looked her up and down "But then I suppose you'd have to think about upping the quality of the merchandise as well." The coat stopped just above her grazed knees also revealing a large ladder in her tights. Her red stilettos were scuffed and battered. Her teeth were turning black and decaying so much she was sure that anyone standing close enough to her could smell it. Sometimes even Lucy wondered why these men paid her for it. They were desperate, she thought, people did disgusting things when they were desperate.

"You got the stuff?" she asked.

He looked around to make sure no one was watching "You got the cash?"

She nodded.

"Cash first" he said.

Reluctantly Lucy released her grip on the flick knife in her pocket. She reached inside her bra and pulled out a handful of crumbled bank notes and handed it to him. All the time his eyes were fixed on hers, staring and never blinking, his mouth closed in a drawn-on smile. He took the money from her and slipped it in to his back pocket. Still he stared and smiled. The sounds of trainers against footballs, prams wheels against pavement began to feel further and further away. Lucy could feel the sweat pouring again, she gasped for air.

"It's all there" she said.

"It's alright I don't need to count it. I know you're not stupid enough to try and cheat me." He took a small package wrapped in tin foil from his inside jacket pocket. He held it up in front of Lucy's face, her heart pounded. Even in the dim light of the alley the package sparkled. Lucy snatched it feverishly. Finally, he broke his stare, the sounds of the street flooded back and Lucy could already feel the calming sensation washing over her. He laughed "Now don't use it all at once. I may be unavailable for a little while."

"What? Why?" she began to panic again.

"I just need to get out of town for a while, lie low, let a bit of heat die down. So, you better be nice to me" He took a cigarette out of his pocket and lit it. He inhaled deeply then leaned back and looked up at the roof of the alley and stared at it as if it were the Sistine Chapel. He leaned forward and blew a large puff of smoke in Lucy's face. She coughed. He smiled his drawn-on smile again, then continued "Or I'll leave you high and dry." He took another drag of his cigarette while with his other hand he reached out and stroked her hair. Lucy flinched; her hand slipped back inside her coat pocket and gripped the knife. "Must dash." He said and turned away, "Work to be done. See you around sweetheart!" he called over his shoulder as he walked back down the alley.

Lucy watched him go; he turned at the end and disappeared. She stuffed the tin foil package inside her bra and wrapped her coat around her tighter, protectively. She turned and marched up the steps. They were hard cold concrete strewn with broken glass, litter and graffiti. She was unbalanced in her high shoes; she almost fell a few times. Her heart was beating heavily but she kept moving as fast as she could. All she could think about was getting back to her flat. She thought about what it would be like, how she was going to feel. She just had to get back there; she just had to keep her feet moving. Lucy barged past anyone who got in her way and gripped her knife tighter.

The lift was broken again. She climbed all fifteen flights of stairs; as she climbed higher and higher, she moved faster and faster. She was breathless, her heart was pounding her limbs were shaking. She reached her front door. The key stuck in the lock. She twisted it, hit it, kicked the door; she could hear herself, her desperate whimpers. Eventually there was a click and the door opened, she was inside.

It was cold and dark; the mould on the walls was starting to smell. Lucy coughed; she walked over to the kitchen table and held on to it to steady herself and get her breath back. She reached inside her bra felt the cold foil and pulled out the package. She held it up and suddenly her little flat seemed beautiful. Lucy shivered as if something had brushed past her;

she looked over her shoulder and turned around quickly. The flat was quiet. There was nothing there. Of course, it was, she shook herself, she just needed a little something then she would be fine.

She went in to the bedroom and sat down on the bed still with her coat wrapped around her. Then she kicked off her shoes. Her feet signed with relief as she placed them flat on to the floor. She reached for the draw by her bed but it was already open. She stopped. I left it like that, she thought. She took what she needed from the draw and closed it again. There was a creek, the sound of a bed spring recoiling. Lucy sat still. Another creek. The mattress sank beneath her; there was the sound of heavy breathing. It was a feeling Lucy was very familiar with. The feeling of someone else getting into bed with her, getting excited. Lucy froze. The sound got closer, and closer, until she could feel the vibrations again her ear and the tiny droplets of saliva on her neck.

Chapter 8

James could feel the office closing in around him. The noise intensified, the constant humming of the printer the ringing of the phones seemed to get louder and louder. It pressed down on his shoulders and his chest until he was gasping for air.

This was the kind of case James had longed for. The kind of case that could make him. He could be a hero. If he succeeded. What if he failed? How long might it take to catch this man? If it was a random killing, stranger murder. They were rare but they did happen and were difficult to solve. If the killer hadn't left any DNA how would they draw up any suspects? And even if he had if he wasn't on the DNA database they'd be just as lost. Random killers didn't normally stop at one murder how many more innocent people might die. The more victims the more attention the case would get.

"Coffee?" Evelyn was there, she placed a steaming mug of coffee down in front of him. He made his composure return, adjusted his tie, swept his hair back into place. He was cocky self-assured, the way he liked everyone to think of him.

"Thanks" he said as he took a sip.

Evelyn perched on the edge of his desk and took of her own coffee, "let's check this out then" she said pointing to the clear plastic evidence bag on James' desk containing the piece of paper found in Jenna Bishop's throat. James nodded and typed in the web address and waited for www.sitbackandwatch.co.uk the first thing that appeared were pictures of Jenna walking to her car, leaving her house. This person had been watching her for a while. Maybe Evelyn was right. This was someone who knew her. He scrolled down to more picture of her getting into her car, clearly taken by someone sitting in the back seat. Then there more taken after her death, different from the police crime scene photos.

"How many people can see this?" James asked as Evelyn leaned closer to the screen.

"It's locked so just us, for now."

"Can we trace this?" he asked.

"It depends, it's easy to be anonymous on line" Evelyn stared into the screen intently.

"Get IT on to this. There must be a way we can find out where this is coming from." James downed his coffee and adjusted his tie.

Chapter

Oscar opened the cupboard and stared inside it. He continued staring for quite a while hoping something would leap out and inspire him. He picked up a tin of corned beef, checked the packaging and realised it was two years past its use by date. He put it back. He stared for a bit longer then opted for beans on toast. He poured the beans in to a bowl and placed them in the microwave. The tea time news chattered away in the living room. It was rare he came home late these days. He would watch the seconds tick by on his computer screen until it turned to five pm. Then he would grab his coat and leave on the dot. In fact, he would quite often leave early and make some feeble excuse to Jean about working from home, which he never did.

The toast popped up. He took it and spread it thickly with butter while the beans still buzzed in the microwave. Something on the TV in the other room suddenly made him listen "A body was discovered at a block of flats today believed to be that of 32-year-old Lucy Maxwell." A picture of a smiling young woman dressed up and ready for a night out appeared on the screen. The news reader continued "Ms Maxwell is thought to have been dead for about two weeks although she had not been reported missing. Her death is being treated as suspicious."

A man appeared on the screen. He was young well groomed, cocky. Oscar thought he had seen him around the station. A caption popped up at the bottom of the picture informing the audience that this man was Detective Chief Inspector James Miller and he was in charge of this investigation. "We are pursuing a number of leads at present however we would urge anyone with information that could help piece together Lucy's last movements to get in touch." He said.

The camera cut back to the news reader in the studio "In other news the last day of the test at old Trafford saw Lancashire…."

The microwave pinged and Oscar went back in to the kitchen. He poured the steaming beans across the toast and found himself thinking about Lucy Maxwell. How could a young woman like that be dead for two weeks and no one missed her? He placed his plate on a tray and carried it in to the living room, sat down in his old battered arm chair and started to eat. Who would notice if he went missing he thought, if he died tonight alone in his house? Would anyone at work notice if he just didn't turn up? He interacted so little with people these days he doubted if he would be missed, not until The Chief called to check his attendance at the monthly budget meeting.

He thought about Lucy. They didn't mention a partner or children. If she was dead in her flat for two weeks with no-one noticing, she must have lived alone. How did she support herself then? Did she work? Did her employer or colleagues not notice she was missing? What about friends? On that photograph she was dressed up going on a night out, she looked happy, Who was she with then? Where were those people now? Didn't they miss her? He stopped himself. He didn't ask the questions anymore. He was biding his time until he retired. Lucy was someone else's problem. Someone else had to think of these questions.

Oscar continues mindlessly shovelling hot beans and toast in to his mouth. He suddenly realised his plate was empty. He placed it down on the floor beside him. Marie hated that. "Take it in to the kitchen," she would say, "I'll load the dishwasher later but don't leave dirty pots in the living room." Marie would never eat her meals in front of the TV. She always set the table and would stay at the table to eat even after Oscar had picked up his plate and taken it in to the living room, but leaving dirty plates on the living room floor was a step too far. "This is not a student house and you are not one of The Young Ones." Oscar could almost hear her voice now, but the house was empty so he leaned back in his chair. It was old, comfy. He had had it so long it had moulded to the shape of his body, no other chair ever felt quite the same. It didn't match the rest of the furniture in the living room. That was leather, chocolate brown with co-ordinating cushions. The armchair had a sort of teal velour floral pattern but the colour had faded and the velour worn down over the years. The armrests were tattered and sagging. It was one of the first pieces of furniture they had acquired when they got married. They didn't have much money then, buy now pay later deals on furniture were few and far between. If you couldn't pay upfront you couldn't have it and furnishing an entire house from scratch wasn't easy on a constable's salary. Their small house contained only a few mismatched basic items that they had purchased second hand or that had been donated to them by friends and family. Oscar had been driving home from work one day when he saw the chair balanced on top of skip outside a house round the corner. He pulled over, looked around to make sure no-one saw him, took the chair and somehow managed to wedge it into the back of his tiny car. He told Marie someone at work was getting rid of it. He knew she wouldn't let him keep it if he told her he took out of a skip. There was nothing wrong with it though. He couldn't understand why someone would throw a perfectly good arm chair away. It had moved with them three times, Marie had tried to convince him to get rid of it when they purchased the chocolate brown leather. "It wouldn't go," she said, "it was old fashioned, it had seen better days." Oscar was having none of it; he would carry out a sit-down protest if he had to. The chair stayed.

Oscar stirred, his neck creaked, he opened his eyes again and it was dark outside. The curtains were open and the orange glow of the streetlight filled the room. He had fallen asleep in his comfy armchair once again. There were many nights where he just stayed there but his neck felt stiff so he decided to take himself up to bed. The TV was still on. A perma-tanned young man was chattering about some lottery draw, 'it must be late,' Oscar thought. He eased himself out of the armchair with a groan, closed the curtains, then turned the TV off. When the darkness and the silence hit him, his thoughts returned to Lucy. He thought of her face in the photograph, then of what her face must have looked like when she was found. He had seen enough dead bodies to piece it together fairly easily. He headed up to bed. Lying still and warm in the dark he did not sleep. He just thought of Lucy's face as he had thought of so many faces before. He couldn't let himself be drawn in to this again. Not now. He was nearly retired.

Chapter 10

The buzzer sounded. Craig Underwood placed the packet of soap powder he was holding back down on the table in front of him. He walked from his work station and once he was clear of the hygiene control area he removed his hair net with a firm tug. The women chattered. They always chattered so inertly. It didn't matter if they were working, drinking, smoking still they chattered. Craig often wondered what they found to talk about. Maybe their lives were just so interesting they couldn't stop supplying information about them, but when Craig listened in, as he sometimes did, it seemed that was most definitely not the case. They mostly complained. They complained about their husbands, boyfriends, and other people's boyfriends they were sneaking around with. They complained about their children. Those who had teenagers complained that they never got out of bed, and those that had toddlers complained that they never slept. They complained about work; about being too tired to do anything when they got home and about not being given enough hours to do at work. When they weren't complaining they were gossiping and passing judgement on the lives of people in Coronation Street and the Kardashians as if these were people they actually knew. If they weren't doing that they were discussing the latest diet fad while shovelling doughnuts in to their mouths.

Craig reached his locker took out his Clingfilm wrapped sandwiches wondering what healthy filling she's tried to enforce on him today and headed for the small canteen. Most people were going outside; he could see them through the open door. There were no windows to the outside in the rest of the factory. The sun was shining probably one of the last nice days before the autumn took hold, Craig chose to stay indoors.

He thought he might be able to get some peace from the women. It was mostly women who worked in the factory. They packed things. They could pack anything that needed packing, toilet rolls, greeting cards, soap, cereal boxes, and pain killers. Today Craig was on soap powder. He stood at a table with a pile of boxes of soap powder in front of him. Somebody further down the line would bend a cardboard pallet and place it on the conveyor belt, and when the pallet passed Craig's table he placed a box of soap powder on it, then as the pallet passed the next two people on the line they did the same. Then the pallet would go through a machine to be shrink wrapped. After that they would be stacked up and taken away to the distribution section. Craig would spend seven and a half hours doing this today. He spent seven and a half hours doing it yesterday and would most likely be spending seven and a half hours doing it tomorrow.

He put some change in one of the vending machines in the canteen and selected a can of coke. People referred to it as the canteen but it was really just a partitioned space in the corner of the factory, with a few grubby tables and chairs and the vending machines. Most people avoided it, choosing instead to eat their lunch outside or sit in their cars if the weather was bad. Craig liked it though; mostly because he knew he would be left alone if he went in there. There were long windows down either side of the canteen, one looked back on to the factory floor and one looked back in to the manager's office, presumably so they could keep watch on everyone from all angles, making sure no was taking longer than they should on their lunch break or sneaking off to make a phone call. There were three vending machines in the canteen, one sold cold drinks, one sold hot drinks and one sold snacks. All were filled with sugar, salt and disappointment.

Craig cracked open his can and took a bite out of his warm sandwich. It was salad. Just salad. He headed back to the vending machine and selected two bags of crisps and chocolate bar, depositing the sandwich in the bin enroute.

Martin came over and sat down with him "Alright Craig?" Martin said chirpily, as he shuffled his chair closer to the table. Martin was short with a slight build. At first glance he could be mistaken for a teenager but up close it became obvious he was in his thirties. He always smiled and was cheery with everyone. He was an idiot, as least Craig thought so. How could anyone work in a place like this, with people like these, and be anything but miserable? They would have to be an idiot, Craig had concluded.

"Alright Martin" Craig mumbled back. He purposely made no effort to endear himself to people and most people ignored him, but Martin always seemed to make the effort to talk to him no matter how many signals Craig gave that he wanted to be left alone.

"How's it going?" Martin said as he sat down on the chair opposite Craig.

Craig looked up from his crisps, the hatefulness in his stare obvious to anyone who saw him, but Martin was busy awkwardly unfolding the paper so he didn't notice. "Oh. It's great. I'm having a fantastic day." Craig said dead pan.

"Oh, that's good" Martin said with a smile.

Idiot, thought Craig.

Martin popped open a bag of crisps and crunched them loudly. He read the paper as he crunched and Craig could hear him mumbling the words out loud. The paper crackled as he turned every page and each time Craig could feel it brushing his hand. He took another vicious mouthful.

"Have you heard about Sharon from distribution?" Martin said.

Craig really did not care about Sharon from distribution, "No." he said flatly.

"She left her husband for Amir, one of the drivers. He's only 22, she's old enough to be his mother." Martin let out a little giggle "I was telling my mum about it, she said 'good for Sharon'." He laughed again. Craig chewed. "Everyone's talking about it, I spoke to Sharon earlier, I was feeling a bit sorry for her, it seemed like people were picking on her and making fun of her but she said she wasn't bothered, that she was happy as she'd ever been and people could gossip as much as they wanted."

"I bet she loves it" Craig muttered.

"What was that?" Martin asked as he popped another large crisp whole in to his mouth and crunched it hard.

"I said I bet she loves it" Craig said loudly as if to drown out the crisp crunching, "She probably thinks she's important now with everyone talking about her, talking about her for doing nothing, but living her life and causing misery to other people to get what she wants. Drawing attention to herself as if that will make her special like the no-mark so-called celebrities that she worships." Craig drew his breath in hard then swallowed. Martin had stopped crunching at least.

Martin turned another page, it crinkled once again. There was silence for a few minutes, Craig was relieved but then Martin spoke.

"Have you seen this in the paper?" Martin asked.

Craig continued eating and didn't even look at the paper "No" he said.

"She only lived a few floors up from us. She was a druggie though, and a prostitute my mum said."

"What?" Craig stopped chewing and looked up.

"This woman who's been murdered, Lucy Maxwell. She lived in the same block of flats as me and my mum." Martin tapped the story on the newspaper in front of him.

"Oh" Craig said turning the paper slightly so he could see the article in more detail "I hadn't heard about it." He shrugged his shoulders.

"She lived a few floors up. I used to see her walking around the estate, always wore a big fur coat even in the summer. 'All fur coat and no knickers' my mum used to say about her. She said she had a lot of men visiting her flat."

Craig swallowed hard "Did she?"

"Hmmm. Yeh. I saw them sometimes; I felt sorry for her really, I didn't think she had much of a family. Mum says the police will find it hard to track down whoever killed her with the amount of different people that passed through that flat."

"Really." Craig sat up straight and stretched his arms out resting his hands behind his head "Is that what the police say, in the article I mean? Is that what it says?"

"It just says they are continuing with their investigation."

Craig nodded silently.

The buzzer sounded again to indicate lunch time was over. Craig put his rubbish in the bin and headed over to his work station.

Chapter 11

Oscar loved his car. It was a 1968 Aston Martin DBS in British racing green. It was reliable and old fashioned but still had a little bit of style. He hated the morning traffic though. Everywhere he went there were road works, the sound of pumping drills, chisels against concrete, muffled gruff workmen's voices and his own grumpy mumblings.

As he stroked the stirring wheel he remembered the day he bought that car. It was a Saturday and it was raining. Marie had gotten up early as she always did. He heard her hoovering downstairs as he dozed with his head buried under the covers. He remembered the sound of the rain battering against the window. He hoped Marie would change her mind about wanting to go out and look for a new car but then he had heard her footsteps on the stairs, heard the bedroom door open, heard the sound of a cup being placed on the bedside table and smelt the bacon in the sandwich that she had brought him. Oscar had never been a morning person but Marie knew once he had breakfast in bed he had no excuse for not getting on with the day. They had been married for five years and Oscar was still driving the Mini Metro he had when he first passed his test. It had a replacement gear stick and a leaking radiator. Marie had insisted they get new car. He was doing well now in the force and he needed to be driving something that reflected his situation, she had told him. Besides they needed something more reliable, with more room. Oscar had gone to the car dealer that day with every intention of buying a grown-up family car but he had fallen in love with the Aston Martin. Marie knew it was foolish. It wasn't big enough and it was too old but she saw his eyes light up. She pretended to be angry but she was always happy to see him happy.

Oscar sat and waited at the latest set of temporary traffic lights. The window was open a fraction; it was a warm day, one of the last thick days of summer. The downside of owning a classic car was that they were made before air conditioning. Heavy grey clouds hung in the sky like a duvet, trapping the last of the sun's warmth close to the ground.

His phone rang; another thing this car did not lend itself too was a hands-free kit. Oscar rummaged around for his phone. He knew he shouldn't answer it but the traffic was stopped any way surely it wouldn't make a difference. It was Jean "Are you nearly here?" she asked.

"I'm stuck in traffic, bloody road works. Hopefully shouldn't be too much longer. Is there a problem?"

"The Chief's been down. She wants to see you."

Oscar paused. The Chief very rarely left her office unless it was to go to a press conference. She certainly didn't wander around the station. Usually she would call or email, if someone was being particularly evasive, as Oscar often was, she would sometimes send one her minions down to summon them. She never went to get them herself.

"Hello? Are you still there?" Jean asked.

"Yes, yes I'm still here" he said "Did she say what she wanted?"

"No, she asked where you were, I said you were probably stuck in traffic."

"Good stuff." Oscar breathed a sigh of relief.

"She didn't seem too happy. She asked me to tell you to go up to her office as soon as you get here. That's why I'm calling." Jean spoke the last few words with the firmness of a headmistress.

Oscar had a habit of lingering around the vending machines, kitchens or anywhere but his office when got in to the building, anything to delay the start of his day for a little longer. He supposed that it was only fair that Jean didn't want to get in to trouble should the chief bump in to him before he'd been given the message.

"I'll make sure I go up to her office as soon as I get there."

"As soon as you get here? "Jean asked although her toned suggested it was more like a command than a question.

The lights changed. Oscar balanced the phone against his ear as he put the car in gear and moved forward. "I promise. I won't even stop for a coffee." The traffic moved but still crawled despite the lights now being green.

"Ok, good. She was pretty insistent."

Jean seemed think Oscar was in some kind of trouble and was worried about being dragged down with him. Maybe he was, he couldn't be sure. He didn't think he'd done anything to draw any particular attention recently but may be his lapse attitude was finally starting to show through.

"Don't worry Jean, I'm sure it's nothing that important. I will go straight up as soon as I'm in the building. You can have a coffee ready for me when I get back down." He laughed.

Jean didn't sound like she was laughing. "I will."

As he rounded the end of the works section the traffic began to flow more freely. Oscar tried to change to second gear but the car stalled and he dropped the phone. He scrambled around trying to locate the phone and start the car again. He held up his hand apologetically. Another car beeped aggressively. He looked up see a woman mouthing the words 'Get off the phone!' at him. A man in the car behind her made a hand gesture; Oscar changed his apologetic hand gesture to mimic that of his fellow road user. The car finally started again, he located the phone and balanced it back next to his ear.

"Hello? Hello? I think you've gone again" Jean was saying.

"No, I'm back. Traffic seems to be moving now. If she gets in touch again just tell her I'm on my way. Goodbye Jean, see you shortly."

"Goodbye." She hung up.

The hum of the radio softened some of the noises from outside. The repetitive jingle signalled the strike of the hour. The news bulletin started. The traffic was moving a steady pace now and Oscar switched on to auto pilot. He had travelled this route so any times now he barely noticed the surroundings, the pedestrians, the other drivers, even his own actions seemed removed from him. He just travelled in a daze.

Chapter 12

It was warm, too warm for Maureen Connolly, and it was very rare that she was warm. Normally she wore at least three layers of clothing and even then, she was still cold. Whenever her daughter came around to visit she would complain about the heat in Maureen's flat. Maureen kept the heating on high most of the time. It was due to her thin blood the doctor had said. It was a good thing, it meant the beta blockers were working and although she shouldn't have any more trouble with her heart, she would feel the cold more. And she did. Maureen dreaded the winter. She felt the cold going through to her bones. Some morning she woke up and thought she had already died. She was that cold she thought she was dead in the morgue. Eventually she gathered the energy to get out of bed, start moving, and slowly things would start flowing. She would feel herself coming back to life.

She didn't know how she got like this. It seemed like only yesterday she was twirling around a dance floor dressed in bright colours covered in rhinestones and feathers her eyes fixed on Stan's, his eyes fixed on her. That was how they met; he turned up at her ballroom dancing class trying to impress a girl. Not Maureen, Barbara Hewitt, but Barbara wasn't interested in Stan she had her eye on Lenny Walters. Lenny had just come back from his National Service in Palestine and was all dark and mysterious and Barbara wasn't about to let anyone else be his partner. She marched right over to Lenny and had him in the midst of an Argentine Tango before he had chance to make any kind of protest. That's when Maureen saw Stan, shuffling in the corner with his hands in his pockets, eyeing up the door desperately. She walked over and introduced herself and asked him to dance. She had never been so forward before but on this occasion, it just seemed right. They danced together all evening. Stan actually turned out to be a pretty good dancer. They entered competitions and won prizes and eventually turned professional. They travelled the world visiting glamorous places in so many glamorous costumes. Eventually they had to grow up, they had a family and the dancing became more of a hobby and eventually fizzled away to a memory. Her life with Stan and their children was still full of sparkle, and smiles and laughter. Yet she missed the dancing. She kept hold off her costumes though hoping maybe one day she would get to wear them again.

Then Stan died. Cancer got him. Robbed him of everything until he was drained and weak and could take no-more. It was the day after his funeral that Maureen got rid of the costumes. The lady in the charity shop looked at her like Christmas had come early. 'Was she really sure she wanted to get rid of them?' The lady had asked. 'They were so beautiful how could she part with them?' Maureen had lost her dancing partner. There would be no more dancing.

Today when she looked in the mirror, if she stared hard enough, she could still see that girl in her dressing room getting ready for a competition; excited, happy, ready to take on the world. If she really looked hard, she could see past the grey hair, the wrinkles, and the tired eyes. She could see that girl full of hope and covered in sparkles.

Maureen stirred the milk and sugar into her tea. She spread the butter and jam on her toast. Same every morning; tea with milk and sugar, two slices of brown toast with butter and strawberry jam. She had been eating this breakfast for as long as she could remember and it had seen her through to eighty-five with only a few bumps in the road. She finished her breakfast and washed the dishes, dried them and put them away. She liked to keep her little flat tidy. Maureen's flat was on the top floor of a fifteen-storey block. There was a leak in the bathroom and mould on the kitchen ceiling. Apparently, there were some loose tiles on the roof above the flat. The lady from the housing association said they were aware of the problem and it was on a list. They would get around to it soon.

Maureen had lived there for 25 years now, since she lost Stan. Her children had convinced her to move, they said the house would be too much for her on her own. Too much cleaning. Maureen didn't mind the cleaning it kept her busy but she felt Stan's absence in every room. It was time for a fresh start. The tower block wasn't exactly picturesque but it had served her well. She knew there was often trouble on the estate but it had never touched her that was until recently. The girl at the other end of the landing, Lucy, had been murdered. She had been at home in her flat too, where she should have felt safe. Mind you, Maureen thought, she was a bit of a wrong 'un, always courting trouble of some kind.

Maureen sat and read her book for an hour. She struggled these days. She needed books in large print and the selection in the library was limited. Her daughter kept nagging her get to get one of those Kindle things but Maureen hadn't been sure. Then last week she was chatting to Betty on the bus and she had one "Oh they're fantastic!" Betty said "I wouldn't be without mine now. I can carry it around in my handbag all day without getting a pain. It's so light you would hardly know it was there. And you can choose whatever size print you want." Maureen had looked on with envy at Betty's little device. She admitted to herself, and to Betty, that day she was keen to have one so she went straight to

Waterstones' and bought one. She didn't want to admit it to her daughter, after all the nagging she had done, but she needed her help to get the thing working. It was still in its box behind the sofa. She would have another go herself at getting it working, maybe this afternoon.

When it got to 11:30 Maureen gathered her things together to head out to Bingo. It was her favourite time of the week, Wednesday Bingo. She loved getting out of the house and catching up with her friends, the few that were still alive. She would often go days without seeing anyone. Her daughter brought her shopping up for her once a week but she never stayed long. She had her own life with a job and a family after all. The rest of her family from her own generation were all gone now, Maureen was the only one left.

A lot of her friends were also gone or in no fit state to climb the fifteen flights of stairs to come and visit her as the lift was broken more often than not. The lift was broken today. Maureen began her decent down the many flights of stairs; she struggled with stairs these days and they made her nervous. He friend Annie had fallen down the stairs two years ago and she had never been the same since, always back and forwards to the hospital with something. That was just the stairs in her house, not fifteen flights of cold concrete.

It was quiet in the stairwell. Maureen was aware of the sounds of her footsteps as she stepped cautiously on each stair they echoed in the empty space. An empty drink can rolled down the stairs next to her, rattling and clattering as it hit each step. Maureen leaned over to try and pick it up and put it in a bin but she was afraid she might lose her balance and fall so she stood up. She took another step. She became aware of another sound. She stopped. She listened. Silence. She took another step down and heard the sound again. Again, she stopped. Again silence. Then it was there, the sound. It was the sound of another set of footsteps. They were behind her; they got closer, and closer.

Chapter 13

Oscar sat on the closest chair to the door. He wasn't sure why, maybe it was because he felt like he always wanted to make a quick getaway whenever he came up against The Chief. She had been drafted in from GMP to steer their little force in the right direction, make sure targets were met, complaints kept down and PR generally improved. These changes had not made her popular with the majority of people at the station, but you can't make an omelette without breaking a few eggs, she would say.

Her office was on the top floor of the station building and was a stark contrast to the rest of the station décor. It had been one of her first tasks when she started the job. She had remodelled half the top floor to accommodate her office. The room, where Oscar was now waiting, was the chief's PA's office. It seemed like a huge space for one person to work in. The PA's desk was on the opposite side of the room to where Oscar sat, it looked old but polished to fit it with its super modern surroundings. Oscar looked down at his scuffed shoes. There were pot plants dotted around the room and inspirational pictures in heavy ornate frames on the walls. The only other furniture was the three chairs where Oscar now sat. They were a rich crimson colour and padded to make them more comfortable than was necessary for a waiting area.

The intercom on the PA's desk buzzed, some words were uttered through it but Oscar couldn't make them out. "Ok I'll send him through" the PA said in to the intercom. She looked up at Oscar, "You can go through now."

"Thanks" Oscar said as he stood up. He adjusted his tie and felt relived he'd chosen today to bother to wear one, his stomach knotted into a half Windsor. He knocked on the heavy oak door that lead into the chief's office.

"Come in" said the voice beyond. Oscar opened the door and stepped inside tentatively. The Chief's desk was directly opposite him in front of a large window and made her look like a bond villain. "Take a seat" she said, motioning to another plush crimson chair in front of her desk. She continued signing papers with a black and gold expensive looking pen. She didn't look up.

Oscar sat down and waited in silence until she had finished what she was doing. Finally, she put down the pen and shuffled the papers in to a neat pile and looked up at Oscar. "How can I help you?" she said.

"You wanted to see me?" he said. He had the sick feeling he remembered from school when he was about to get into trouble. He had to remind himself that he didn't care.

"Ah yes" she said "How are things?"

Oscar felt confused "Things are fine," he said puzzled.

The Chief smiled at him, it looked like it caused her pain "Things at home ok?"

What kind of question was that? Oscar thought there wasn't much at home to cause him either issues or happiness and she knew that. "Yes." He said. "Things are fine."

"You're a keen gardener, aren't you?" she said.

"Erm no, not particularly." Now he was really confused. The closest he's ever got to gardening was running a mower over the lawn now and again after being nagged into it. Where was she getting this from?

"I heard your vegetables had won prizes"

"Ah, no." Oscar said "That was my wife's domain. Her vegetable patch was her pride and joy."

"I see" said the Chief. She shifted uncomfortably in her chair then took out her expensive looking pen again circled something on a piece of paper. Feeding her miss-information, someone was going to be in trouble. She sat up straight again and rolled back her shoulders "Somewhat of a jungle then now is it, the vegetable patch?"

"Yes, yes it most definitely is I'm afraid. I don't have my wife's talent for gardening."

"Oh no there's nothing to it really, no talent involved. It just takes a bit of dedication that's all, a bit of time, but then time is a great luxury to us all isn't it?" she smiled again, Oscar didn't like it.

"It is indeed" he said.

"I bet you'd love a little more time on your hands, really get to grips with that garden, restore it to its former glory."

"Well possibly" Oscar said "I hadn't really given it much thought, may be when I retire."

The Chief held up a finger as if something had occurred to her, just then in that very moment. "I was wondering if you might be interested in this" she reached inside a draw and took out a spiral bound booklet and handed it to Oscar, the words 'Early Retirement Options' were written on the front of it.

"I don't understand" said Oscar, "I am retiring, in six months."

"Yes, we know, but we thought you might like to consider going a little earlier? "she smiled like a game show host.

Who is 'we,' Oscar thought. He looked back down at the booklet, he had been counting the days until he could take his retirement but the now the prospect was closer, imminent even, suddenly he felt uneasy.

"You don't have to make a decision now" The Chief said "just have a read through it and get back to me. Think of the garden. You could get it into great shape in no time." She smiled.

He now realised why she had chosen to see him in person. She wanted to give him a nudge, make sure he got the message, he was past it and it was obvious. It was a nudge to leave early, to get out of the way and she wanted to make sure he knew this nudge came from the top. "I'll have a look through it" he said with a fake smile. "Was that everything?"

The Chief continued smiling back, she was just as fake as he was "Yes." She said "Yes that's everything. You just get back to me when you're ready, but don't take too long." She said firmly.

"I won't" Oscar said and stood up to leave the room. The Chief stood up too and reached out to shake his hand. He felt like he was already being waved off.

He walked slowly back through the PA's grand office and down the corridor to the lift. Once inside he leaned back against the wall and looked at booklet. He flicked through a couple of pages. Maybe it was for the best, he thought, maybe he should just go now.

Chapter 14

Oscar sat and stared out of the window of his little office. He watched the tree outside swaying in the breeze. Its leaves were starting to turn orange and red. It wouldn't be long until they withered and fell to the ground to rot. He picked up his coffee cup and took a sip. It was stone cold. He winced and put it back down again. The rest of the office was quiet. It was Friday and most people had made excuses to leave early, just a handful remained hidden behind their computer screens either catching up on work they had already completed or putting off going home. Oscar fell in to both categories. He had no interest in his work anymore, spending most of his days in his little office trying to avoid speaking to anyone. They all thought he was working but most of the time he was just playing games on his computer or staring aimlessly out of the window. He didn't want to go home either, not today. Unlike most people, Fridays were the days he dreaded. Nothing but a long, lonely, weekend in front of him. He thought again about his retirement.

He opened a draw in his desk. The booklet The Chief had given him stared up. He still hadn't read it. He went to pick it up but changed his mind and closed the draw again. There was a time when he dreaded going home because he couldn't switch off from the job. He would feel restless, agitated. He couldn't sleep, he lost the ability to sit down and enjoy a proper meal. He always preferred to be working. Often, he would get up in the middle of the night and go to his study and send emails, reply to emails, go over evidence. Then he began bypassing domestic pleasantries all together. As soon as he was through the door he would just go straight to his study and carry on working. That was if he bothered to come home at all. He was free to do whatever he wanted now. Only now he hated it.

He hated the silence more than anything. Even in the times when he had been engrossed in his work he would hear Marie downstairs, pottering around, hoovering, talking to her sister on the phone. Now there was nothing but the silence. It gave him too much time to think; he craved distraction but it would never come.

He went to the little office kitchen to make more coffee. He couldn't face going home yet. Arthur was in there, stirring his coffee and sloshing it all over the worktop while he read the paper. Oscar thought about going back to his desk to avoid a conversation but Arthur had already seen him "Alright Gov?" Arthur said.

"Evening Arthur." Oscar put his cup down and flicked the kettle on, "You working late too?" He knew he had to make some effort at conversation.

"Paperwork" said Arthur, rolling his eyes and taking a slurp of coffee "You in the same boat?"

Oscar placed a teaspoon of instant coffee in a mug "Yes, yes it's never ending." The kettle boiled and he poured the water in the mug. He couldn't look at Arthur. The truth was all he ever did these days was paperwork but due to the fact he had been playing computer games and starring out of the window most of the day he was massively behind.

Arthur picked up the paper and started reading it, so much for catching up on paperwork, thought Oscar. "Could be worse" Arthur said, "I hear the Murder Squad are having a tough time of it."

"Really?" said Oscar.

"Yeh, that James Miller" Arthur made a face "And his team. The Chief has been on their backs about it. Not even got one suspect for any of them apparently." He drank his coffee while staring at the paper,

"Golden Boy must be losing his shine, and it looks like it's about to get worse. There's been another."

Oscar dropped his spoon, "What? When?" he said.

"Wednesday afternoon, little old lady apparently. Here." Arthur handed Oscar the paper "Strange though isn't? In a small place like Hoddlesworth? Murders are mostly just domestic, open and shut. Unusual to have three unsolved cases in just a few weeks?"

"Yes" said Oscar.

"Maybe that Miller's not quiet the superstar he's made out to be."

"What kind of superstar?"

"The Chief poached him from GMP, used to be in vice. Supposedly one of the youngest officers to make DCI. My theory is they want him fast tracked, got him heading up the murder squad because it's easy. So he gets good results and everyone thinks he's a superstar."

"Yeh I think have seen him around."

"You will have, cocky bugger, walks around like he owns the place."

Arthur took another slurp of coffee and looked at his watch. He sighed "You know, it wasn't long ago when by this time on a Friday I'd be warming up with a few pints before wearing out the dance floor until two in the morning. Now I'm here, still slogging away before going home to the wife and screaming kids."

Oscar looked at him, "Don't knock it" he said as he stirred the milk into his coffee.

Arthur shrugged "Yeh I know, anyway best get back to it," he nodded towards the door "See you later Gov." He was gone.

Oscar didn't want to read the story in the paper Arthur had given him but he couldn't help himself. That was the third since the start of September; all in the same little town. Arthur was right it was strange, but Oscar didn't share Arthur's theory about the murder squad just being incompetent. There was more to it than that. Surely there had to be a connection between the murders? Oscar put the paper back on the table turning it around so he couldn't see the rest of the article but not before flicking through it to see if there had been an update on the Worthington Farm story, there was nothing. Oscar put the paper down and walked back to his office.

Chapter 15

It was still warm. Craig battled with his shopping trolley, one of the wheels kept spinning the opposite way to the way he was pushing it, and then it would stick there. He turned in to the dairy aisle; the chill from the fridges was a welcome relief from the muggy heat outside. It was noisy. They didn't play music anymore but the aisles were filled with the constant chatter of shoppers occasionally interrupted by the overly cheerful ramblings of the announcer who stood at the front of the store, often in a stupid costume, announcing the latest deals over the loud speaker.

Craig took his phone out of his pocket and checked the shopping list his wife had sent him via text message earlier that day. He called her as soon as he was on his lunch break and explained why he couldn't do it. He was tired, it was Friday and he was already working overtime. Plus he had other things to do that evening. She said she was tired too. She had things to do and he was selfish; she never asked him to do anything...eventually Craig gave in and did what she asked. He went to the supermarket after work to get the shopping.

Low fat yoghurts were next on the list, he saw a blue tub that said yoghurt and put it in the trolley without bothering to check if it was low fat or not. "She'd stuff a cream cake down her throat quick enough," he thought, "what was she so bothered about low fat yoghurt for?"

He carried on walking down the aisle when woman in front of him stopped suddenly. Craig's mind was miles away and he bumped his trolley in to her legs.

"Ow! Watch it!" she said.

"Me watch it?!" Craig said, his heart was suddenly beating fast and he could feel his face turning red, "Why don't you watch it!" he was shouting now "You just stopped right in front of me!" People had stopped what they were doing and were staring at them.

The woman looked at the floor, her cheeks flushed "Alright" she said "Just be more careful" she glanced round at the other shoppers and moved to one side.

Craig carried on forwards with his trolley; he heard one of the other shoppers, an old lady with a shopmobilty scooter, 'tut' loudly as he passed. His hands gripped the trolley tighter but he bit his tongue.

His phone rang in his pocket. He knew who it would be and that there was no point letting it go to voicemail as she would only keep on ringing. He took his phone out and saw his wife's picture, a misleadingly flattering photograph she had chosen, flash up on the screen. There was a long silence at Craig's end before he was given the chance to speak. "Yes, I know…I'm here now…yes I got yoghurt…quark? What's that?.like cheese….well I've already been…ok…ok fine….I'll go back. Right …yeh, I know…. I'll be as quick as I can." He shoved his phone back in his pocket and turned the trolley around. The wheel stuck again so he shoved it and marched back down the aisle. The woman who had tutted at him earlier whizzed past the end of the aisle on her scooter and gave him a filthy look. The wheel stuck again, Craig pushed the trolley forward but it only moved a few inches before it stuck another time. Craig kicked the wheel, and then kicked it again, and again, until the trolley tipped over. The not low-fat yoghurt split open as it hit the floor covering the rest of the goods in white goo. The woman on the scooter had stopped and was turning around. Craig kicked the broken yoghurt pot so it made more mess flying up in the air, splattering what was left of its contents all around it. The woman on the scooter shook her head. Craig marched out of the supermarket without looking at anyone, leaving the shopping where it was on the floor.

Chapter 16

Elaine Chase had been an educator for over 28 years. She had been the first person in her family to get a degree and had worked in teaching since she graduated. She had never wanted to do anything else. The youngest of four and the only girl, her family were stunned when she went away to university. Some of them said they were proud but most of them told her it was a waste of time. They thought she was just mucking around for three years instead of getting a job and paying her way. She did get a job and pay her way; she worked in a pub and supermarket and took on various seasonal jobs in shops and garden centres. She worked hard and she had continued working hard ever since. She was proud of what she had achieved.

It had been five years since her father's stroke. The rest of the family had assumed she would naturally give up her job and take care of him, since her mother was in no fit state anymore. She was bad with arthritis and her heart had seen better days. Elaine refused, she found the suggestion utterly ridiculous. She was the only who had a good job so why should she be the one to quit? It didn't go down too well - when it came to her father's funeral nobody spoke to her.

Elaine had been the headmistress of Church Road Primary School for the last fifteen years. She had taken the school from Special Measures to being classed as Outstanding by Ofsted. Parents moved house or lied about where their children lived in order to get a place at Elaine's school. The staff and pupils had mixed feelings about her. She was firm but fair; she didn't enter the teaching profession to be liked after all. Her methods got results and that's what mattered.

She had spent the last hour walking around the empty school building. The oppressive heat of the day was starting to fade, the cool evening air signalling the oncoming of autumn. The smells of chalk, marker pens and paper felt like tonic to her. This is where she belonged; this is what she was meant for.

On Monday a new week would start and these classrooms would be filled with the sounds of chatting, laughter, scraping chairs and shouting voices.

Elaine went outside and worked her way around the perimeter. She stood in the street looking at the newly painted red railings and the school beyond. It was quiet without the children; not just the school but the street seemed quiet too. A can blew in the wind; it rattled and rolled along until it reached Elaine's feet. She bent down and picked it up. As she straighten up she looked ahead and saw her shadow, it was strange blurred at the edges as though someone else was standing behind her.

Chapter 17

The air was thick and heavy. Oscar sat in his car with the windows down but still he felt like he couldn't breathe. He looked at the hazy red traffic light in front of him and only became aware it had changed when a driver behind him beeped angrily. He held up his hand in the rear-view mirror apologetically and drove on. He wasn't sure where he was going to; he just knew he didn't want to go home. He kept driving. He kept driving until the lights and the noise of Hoddlesworth were far behind him. He suddenly felt very tired. He had not had a good night's sleep in years but he was tired in general - tired of thinking, tired of remembering. He had been counting down the days until his retirement. He started to think about why. What was he going to do with himself anyway? Sit alone with his thoughts? Play chess?

The road underneath the tyres turned from solid concrete to grinding dirt. He stopped the car and got out. He knew this place. He was high up on a hill. The road ended and pooled out to a rough-edged car park that filtered down to wild moorland grass and trees. He would come here with Marie when they first started dating. Then later they would walk here. There were footpaths that lead off in to the woods. Sometime they would bring a picnic, sit on one the benches and enjoy the view. Marie made no secret of her desire for a dog to give them more reason to come up and walk here but Oscar never felt it was the right time. They also talked of bringing grandchildren here, but that never happened either.

Tonight, there was no view, only darkness. The spot looked down on a disused quarry now filled with water. There were a number of signs along the road on the way up warning people not swim in the water, on a danger of death. Oscar walked to the edge; it was a long way down. In the darkness the water merged with the rest of the blackness. It was so quite here, so empty. Oscar took a step closer to the edge. He closed his eyes and searched for Marie's face but he couldn't find it. The only face he saw was Carrie's, like always. For twenty years she had been there never letting him rest. He could make it stop now though, he thought. Right now, tonight he could make it all stop. The memories, the regrets, they would all just go away. Somewhere in the distance there was a rumble of thunder. He looked up hoping to see stars and bask in moonlight but there was nothing but darkness above him, the thick clouds keeping the stars covered. It started to rain. He felt a heavy drop land on his face, smelt the damp air around him. He took another step forward.

Chapter 18

3rd September 1995

The windows were still closed, strange, she thought on such warm day. The air was thick, she felt the dust and salt on her tongue. It was the first day of term; she walked home slowly thinking of the summer just gone. Long lazy days, barbeques and ball games until the sun finally went down long in to the day. They had been away on holiday, camping in Wales, same place they went every year but she loved it there. They had been going every summer for as long as she could remember. Green fields that stretched down to the beach, the little pub they always played Pool in, eating fish and chips off the same little wall down by the harbour whilst fighting off seagulls. She didn't care that her friends went abroad, Spain, Tenerife, they could keep it.

Her house was at the end of a long lane. It had once been a working farm, an arable farm; she remembered the barley smell, her mother used to make her own barley water cordial. Her father would be out in the fields all day. He sat down to dinner in the evening smelling of dirt and hard work. It wasn't easy making money from farming though. After her mother died he seemed to lose any fight that had been left in him and gradually the land had been sold off bit by bit. Now all that was left was the house and the garden and a small vegetable patch. The land surrounding them was covered with orange and white box houses.

Walking down that lane though she could still pretend she was away from it all. The lane was a dirt track two lines of dust and stones with a line of over grown grass in between. Along each side there were thick lines of trees that thankfully blocked out the houses behind. Today they were providing some much-needed shade, the sun danced between the pink petals of the cherry blossoms. The lane turned at the end and revealed the house. It was detached and perfectly symmetrical with a faded wooden door, the bright red paint long since peeled away. Either side of the door was a sash window. The windows would rattle in the wind, the timbers had long since rotted and crumbled. There were gaps in the roof where some of the slates had fallen off, sometimes the rain seeped through and ran down the bedroom walls and through the kitchen ceiling. Her father's old green Land Rover was parked outside, mud splattered as though it might be about to take root. Like the rest of the house it had seen better days, "Like me" her father would say. After the farm had been sold he had to take work as a builder. The money still wasn't great but at least it was regular. That is what he would say anyway, but she got the impression he was trying to convince himself more than the rest of them. These days he ate his dinner alone in front of the TV he smelt of dirt and disappointment. She saw him sometimes staring out of the window across at the houses; she could see him picturing the way it used to be the fields, the crops. It was as if a speech bubble hovered above his head asking, 'Have I done the right thing?'

She put her key in the door but it opened as soon as she leaned on it. It was dark inside, all the curtains were drawn, maybe it was because of the heat? Someone had told her they did that in Spain, kept the curtains drawn on hot days to keep the house cool. It was quiet. It was never quiet in their house. Her father remarried seven years ago and she now had three younger brothers who were constantly playing and fighting and kicking footballs.

There was always the sound of something breaking or crashing, the sound of her stepmother yelling at them to stop what they were doing and take that outside, her father's voice booming occasionally interrupting and echoing her stepmother's sentiments. Things would hush slightly, for a while, then the volume would steadily increase and the process would start all over again. She knew it so well, now it was gone it seemed she only really noticed it for the first time.

"Hello!" she called in to the dark quiet house. There was no reply.

She walked in to the hallway; she became aware of the ticking clock on the wall behind her. She looked down at the wooden floor where two rectangles of light from the frosted glass in the door were cast beside her battered plimsolls.

"Hello?" she called again. Still no reply.

She threw her school bag down, it landed with a thud. She looked in to the living room. The curtains were drawn. The furniture was where it had always been, the cushions on the couch were neat, perfect. She swallowed hard. She wanted to call out again but suddenly she felt unable to. She walked in to the kitchen, the blinds were pulled down but the door leading out to the garden was open. It blew in the wind and tapped against the frame. The table was set for three, tuna sandwiches cut in to triangles, the crusts removed. One sandwich had a bite taken out of it. There was juice in the plastic cups, all at different levels and a half drunken cup of tea at the counter where her stepmother would sit. She put her hand on the cup, it was cold. The chairs were all tucked under the table neatly.

She walked up the stairs, they creaked with each step. The clock still ticked. A fly buzzed. She went in to her room. Her bed was made; cushions were placed on it, just as she had left them. She walked over to the window and opened the curtains. The garden was just like it always was, the wind was still. She turned around and closed an open draw in her dressing table. Did I leave it like that? She thought.

Next, she went in to her parents' room. She saw them. Just shapes it seemed huddled together on the bed, the five of them. Her urge call out died. She walked around the bed. Through her plimsolls she could feel the damp; the carpet was wet with something. She stood by the window with her back to them. Her fingers touched the hem of the curtains. She held them there for a second. Then she pulled the curtains open.

Chapter 19

Oscar leaned back in the driver's seat and took a deep breath. He gripped the steering wheel hard as if making sure it was still real, that he was still real. The storm had broken and the rain was beating down. Flashes of lightening lit up the quarry below. His arms ached. He rotated his ankle; it felt sore. He looked down at the mud and grass on his coat and started to laugh. He wasn't sure why, he just felt like laughing. The windows of the car were still down and the air smelt fresh and clean. The steering wheel felt cold beneath his wet fingers and he was relieved. For the first time in years he felt relieved to be taking another breath. Carrie had been there the whole time and he couldn't leave her, not until he worked it out. He started the car and drove back down the hill towards the town.

The lights grew brighter and warmer. The rain was driving down hard. People ran from shop doorways to cars desperately clutching umbrellas or holding newspapers over their heads in a vain attempt to protect themselves from the deluge.

Oscar drove through the streets with the other cars, the traffic now diluted. There were some people standing at a bus stop. Oscar noticed none of them was wearing headphones which he thought was strange as you didn't see that very often these days. There was a boy who looked to be in his late teens who stood holding his phone resting against his chin, ready to make a call. A woman who looked to be in her early 40's with her arms folded tight across her chest and a man who looked older with greying hair with his hand in his coat pockets constantly shifting his weight from one foot to the other. He kept looking around. They all kept looking around. They're scared, thought Oscar.

Through the rain he saw the glow of lights from a fish and chip shop. That had been their Friday ritual, fish and chips. That was the only time Marie didn't set the table. They would sit on the sofa and eat the fish and chips straight out the paper with little wooden forks. Oscar pulled over went inside the chip shop and joined the queue. The air smelt of vinegar. The queue of people moved forward shuffling their shoes between the sounds of shovelling of chips on metal spatulas and the crinkling of chip paper. Oscar stood beside the glass fronted heaters and embraced the warmth.

He placed his order "Five minutes on fish love" the woman behind the counter said.

"No problem" said Oscar and handed over his money. As he did so he noticed his hands, there was mud and grass still under his finger nails where he had scrambled back up the bank. Had he really come that close?

He leaned against the tiles on wall. The woman took a piece of fish and sluiced it in batter, then placed it in the deep fat fryer. It sizzled. A television on the wall chattered in the background "Police are appealing for information in the murder of primary school head teacher Elaine chase. Ms Chase's body was discovered earlier this afternoon outside the school where she worked. It appears she had been stabbed police are urging anyone with information to contact them."

"You want salt and vinegar love?" asked the woman behind the counter.

Oscar's eyes were fixed on the television screen "What?" he said, "Oh yes please, plenty of it."

She obliged and wrapped the fish and chips with a smile "There you go love" she said.

"Thank you" he found himself smiling genuinely, he couldn't remember the last time he did that. He took the fish and chip bundle, and a wooden fork, to his car.

He unwrapped them and ate them straight away despite his dirty hands. His mind was on Elaine Chase and the other recent murders. The details began to flood his brain.

Chapter 20

The engine hummed. Levi Archer looked down at the clock; he'd been waiting five minutes already. He hadn't set the meter running yet; he didn't like to do that. A lot of his colleagues turned the meter on as soon as they arrived at the fare but Levi thought it was a bit harsh. Sometimes people were running late. Sometimes they had a crisis to deal with at the last minute. The other drivers called him soft but he liked to think of himself as kind. Five minutes was a long time though. He touched the crucifix that dangled from his rear-view mirror and sighed. Another couple of minutes, then he would start the meter. Levi yawned; it had been a long day. By day he worked as a printer and a mini cab driver by night, but it wouldn't be for much longer. He had nearly saved enough. He looked at the photographs on his dash board and touched the faces of his grandchildren. He had only ever seen them on Skype. He understood why they had wanted to go; the cost of living was lower, there was more sunshine, more opportunities for the children to get outside and be healthy and active. If Levi had had that opportunity when his children were young he probably would have taken it. It was so far away though.

There had barely been any days that summer that had been bright. They had all seemed grey and overcast and disappointing. Soon it would be dark when he left in the morning, dark when he left his first job and dark as he worked through his second. Levi had been working two jobs for the last three years to save up enough money to go and visit his family. He had priced up a plane ticket, and in just three more weeks and he would be able to go and book it. Escaping the winter and traveling to the other side of the world where the sun shone. He had thought about not coming back. There wasn't much here for him now since Corrine left.

She had traded him for sunshine too; a Turkish waiter she met on girls' holiday. The waiter was twenty years younger than her but they were in love, apparently. She'd gone away and never come home, why couldn't he? The winter felt worse as he got older. With each year his bones ached more and his chest grew heavier. He would have to come home though; they had a points system to decide if you would be allowed to stay. He had already worked his score out on a website. He was too old. Too old to enjoy the sun, too old to enjoy his grandchildren. He would have to come back but he would face that worry later. For now his was counting his money and counting down his last three weeks until he could book his ticket.

He heard a door open. A woman appeared, smartly dressed, with neat hair that blew in the wind and seemed to distress her. She wore a dusky pink Mac which she wrapped around her tightly. She opened the door and got in to the back seat placing a small wheeled suitcase on the seat next to her.

"Sorry to keep you waiting" she said "Nightmare evening. Traffic was terrible and I didn't get in until gone six and then...oh well I'm ready now."

"Not to worry love." Levi said with a sympathetic smile "Where we off to?"

"The train station please."

"Right you are."

Levi started the car the woman sat with her hands clutching her handbag, which was also a dusky pink, and stared out of the window. Most people these days played with their phones, or tablets or laptops. They seemed to have lost the ability to sit still along with the art of conversation. Levi felt they put a wall up to put him off talking to them. There was a time when a cab drivers' conversational skill was reflected in his tips.

He decided to try conversation with this one "You going anywhere nice?" he asked.

"Not really" she said "My mother in-law had a fall. I'm going to visit her"

"Oh, dear I'm sorry to hear that my dear."

"Which part? The bit about her having a fall or the part about me going to visit her?" she smiled wickedly, "I know which bit I'm sorry about" she muttered.

Levi laughed "Ah she can't be that bad?"

"She can. Injury or no injury she'll still summon up the energy to tell me how terrible my hair looks, how much weight I've put on and what I terrible cup of tea I've made. That woman was born evil."

"Ah now, I don't believe anyone is born evil." Levi said. "Sometimes I think there are people who have had such a terrible time in life they don't understand what it is to be happy. "

The woman looked back at him like she was thinking about what he said.

"And of course, there are some people who are just rude" Levi said with a shrug and a smile. The woman raised her eyebrows and smiled back "I think the best way to deal with them is to be extra nice. Shame them in to being nice back," he continued.

"Hmm" she said "I'll try."

They approached the station and she got out taking her little suit case with her. Levi was about to offer to lift it for her but she seemed to manage it easily.

"That'll be £6.80 please love."

She handed Levi a ten-pound note "Keep the change" she said "Thank you for the advice. I'll try my best to remember it."

"You're very welcome my dear. Thank you very much".

She turned and walked in to the train station wheeling her suitcase behind her. Levi folded the money and placed it in the lock box "And good luck with your mother-in-law" he called after her, but she had gone.

Levi smiled to himself as he drove off. He was pleased there were still some nice people in the world. He pulled up at a set of traffic lights. The passenger door opened, he was about to speak when he felt the cold steel press against his temple. He froze and looked straight ahead.

"Just drive" the voice said.

Chapter 21

There was a knock at the door. The caller did not wait to be invited in but twisted the handle within seconds of the knuckles on his other hand leaving the glass. Oscar has seen him before, he recognised him from the TV appeal for information on death of Lucy Maxwell and he had seen him around the station, he knew his name but he had never spoken to him. Oscar didn't need to speak to him. He may not know this guy personally but he knew his type and that was enough. He had seen them come and go over the years. Many had risen above him, many bottled it when they came to realise just how much nastiness there was in the world. These were the ones Oscar really hated. The ones who could walk away, immerse themselves in a shiny plastic reality; spreadsheets, soap operas, pension plans, penalty shoot outs, company cars and cannelloni. Oscar didn't understand how people could become interested in these things, become enthralled by them; lose sleep over them, write blogs about them, as though these were things that really mattered. As though putting up this smoke screen of modern living would make the evil just go away.

Standing before Oscar was the latest in this batch. Smart suit, three piece, expensive, flashy, too much for everyday work attire. Hair – cut often, styled, possibly highlighted and filled with product.

James walked through the door and offered his hand to Oscar "DCI James Miller, a pleasure to finally meet you sir, mind if come in?" James said as he shut the door behind him. Oscar minimised the contents of his screen as James pulled up a chair.

"Be my guest." Oscar replied "What can I do for you?"

James leaned back in his chair making his fingers in to a steeple formation "Oh no sir, I think the question is what I can do for you?"

Oscar said nothing. A few seconds passed. James cleared his throat and adjusted the knot in his tie "I have a case...a number of cases I think you might be interested in, a series of murders."

Oscar felt the hairs on his neck prickle, he had thought of nothing else since the night at the quarry. Did he still have it in him to get involved with something like this? Now? he wasn't' sure.

"You are talking serial killer?" Oscar said trying to sound nonchalant.

"Possibly .... But there are variations, so it's difficult to be sure" said James, the pause made Oscar wonder if he too was trying to come across more confident than he really was.

"Weapon?"

"Different each time"

"Victim - old? young? Male? Female?"

"Again, it varies"

"Connection to the victim? MO?"

"I'm working on that"

Oscar leaned back in his chair and looked at his pen as he moved it through his fingers, "So what you are telling me is you have series of murders using different weapons, on different victims, with no connections and you want me to help you catch a serial killer?" He looked back up at James.

James shuffled in his seat "I know it seems unlikely and it doesn't fit with any profiling technique used previously but these cases are linked, I'm sure of it"

Suddenly it all felt too big, too varied, too difficult. Oscar saw Carrie's face remembered his broken promises. He couldn't face that again.

"Go see HR, get them to book you in on a profiling course. Your basic skills obviously need some polishing" Oscar said turning his back to James and fiddling with his computer.

James stood up "I came to see you because I heard you used to be good" Oscar flinched "Like a dog with a bone, they used to say about you" James ran his hands through his hair; his suit seemed to crumple "You know what though; people don't say that about you anymore. They say you've given up. Just eking out your time until you can claim your big fat pension. Suit yourself. You keep pen pushing and leave the real detective work to the rest of us." He stood up and walked towards the door.

Oscar began to open files as though James had already left. James waited a moment, exasperated, hoping for a reply. It did not come.

He opened the door abruptly but only got one foot through it before he turned back and closed the door again "He sends a message" James said "After each of these killings there's a message. A calling card if you like." Oscar's eyes flickered but he said nothing.

James opened the door again to leave, "What does it say?" Oscar asked.

"It's a blog. Like he's documenting a hobby." Oscar turned his chair back to face James, "It's not gone public, yet, all the murders are on there. There must be a connection, something we're missing."

"Killers who leave clues usually want to be caught. They crave attention, they want to prove how clever they are, have potential victims running scared."

"You know I'm on to something. I know you do. It doesn't fit, it doesn't make sense but it's all connected. It all means something and you're dying to figure it out as much as I am. "

Oscar turned back to his screen "Like I said, go and see HR"

James stood to leave again. He knew he was going this time but before he did he took a memory stick from his pocket and threw it onto Oscar's desk "Just in case your curiosity gets the better of you. The case files are on there." James left the office without looking back. Oscar sat in his threadbare chair with the memory stick beside his hand on the desk.

He went back to the file he had been working on when James came in -news clipping from the recent murders. He was sure James was right, there had to be a connection. It was exactly what he had been thinking too.

Chapter 22

Isobel Montgomery-smith was 64. She had never married. She had no children. Her mother had loathed her father and his intolerably common surname hence Isobel's double barrel.

Instead of having a family, Isobel had devoted herself to the church and the parish community. She was chair of the Friends of the Library, secretary on the committee of the little theatre and a member of the WI.

Isobel lived alone, still in the red brick terrace house she used to share with her parents. They were now gone.

It was Friday. Isobel had been to set up the flowers at the church for a wedding the following day. It was already dark when she left the church. The heavy oak door thudded shut and she locked it as she always did. In the church yard the wind rustled through the trees. The graves in the churchyard were all very old. They didn't bury people there anymore and those already in residence did not have anyone left to tend their graves or bring flowers. Anyone who could remember them when they were alive was now long since dead themselves. Some of them occupied the graves with their relatives; some were alone except for the moss that encroached on the tombstones.

Isobel had studied the graves many times. She liked to take an interest in them as no-one else did and she felt sorry for them. She had looked many of them up on the census; what job they did, how many children they had, where they lived. It should not be as though they had never existed just because there is no one here now who remembers them, she thought.

Tonight, she kept her hood up as she walked through the church yard. She closed the gate behind her and walked across the road to the bus stop. The road was quiet. There was the rattle of the paper boy's trolley as he reluctantly pulled his cart along the row of houses on the other side. A strong gust of wind blew. There was a squeak of rusty hinges the clatter of iron against stone. Isobel looked across the road at the gate to the church yard; it was swinging in the wind. She tugged at the crucifix on its chain around her neck. "I closed the gate," she thought, "Didn't I?" The paper boy had disappeared around the corner but Isobel could still hear the rattle of the trolley. The street was empty now; she was alone standing at the bus stop, the rattle of the paperboy's trolley growing fainter.

Isobel was about to cross the road to close the gate when something startled her. The beam of headlights, a hiss of breaks as the bus trundled down the road and lurched to a stop beside her. She looked back at the swinging gate, "Won't do any harm for one night," she thought. She stepped aside to allow a woman with some large shopping bags to climb down, "Thank you" the woman mumbled. Isobel fumbled around in her bag for her bus pass as she climbed on to the bus. She almost didn't notice the man in the hooded jacket brush past her, quickly showing his ticket to the driver and making his way to the back of the bus.

The lights of the evening blurred past the windows as the bus made its way through the town, Isobel shivered, something made her jerk her head back to look behind her, the seat was empty. The window above it was open; Isobel stood up steadying herself carefully so she did not fall on the moving bus and closed the window. She sat back down and rubbed her arms to warm up.

The bus ground to a stop at the end of Isobel's street. A couple of other people got off at the same stop, they turned on to the main road which leads back towards the town. Isobel crossed the road and walked down her street, the street she had been walking down all her life. It was a street like many other in this part of the world. It sloped down a hill with rows of red brick Victorian terraced houses facing each other on either side. They were larger than most with big bay windows surveying the street from the ground floor, some from the first floor too. The street was empty. Isobel's house was right at the bottom end; it overlooked a wooded area where the railway used to run. Half way down there was a cross roads. The last house on the end of that row had been a pub, the Kings Arms, for as long as Isobel could remember. Her father used to drink in there often, much to her mother's annoyance. Isobel passed the pub and walked to the edge of the kerb and stopped. She looked both ways although there was hardly ever any traffic passing through. She then turned to look behind her. The street was empty. Isobel crossed the road, adjusted the strap of her handbag on her shoulder and felt the need to walk a little bit faster. Next door's black cat was waiting on the gate post as always. Isobel wanted to stroke him but her allergies wouldn't allow it.

Isobel had never gotten used to the feeling of coming home to an empty house. "You should get timers for your lights when you're out and about," Mrs Johnston from next door had told her, "Especially with the darks nights coming, when the house is in darkness early in the evening it's obvious no-one is home." Isobel knew she was right but she was not great with modern technology so she decided against timers and came home to a dark house instead.

She turned the key in the lock. It clicked with a familiar sound. She wiped her feet on the mat like always, opened the door to the vestibule, hung her coat on the pegs at the bottom of the stairs, placed her handbag next to it, like always. The door to the lounge was closed. She didn't open it. As she entered the kitchen she shuddered again. She checked the heating, and it felt warm. It was late. She made herself some warm milk and honey then headed up to bed. She still slept in the small bedroom at the back of the house. It had been ten years since her father died, her mother followed him five years later but Isobel had never been able to bring herself to move into the large bedroom at the front that had been theirs. It just felt wrong somehow.

Isobel changed in to her nightie, turned the little lamp on by her bed and got under the covers. Holding the novel, she was reading in one hand and her mug of hot milk in the other, she was happily engrossed in her book while sipping her hot milk, when she heard a noise outside. Like something falling over. She put her book down and looked out of the window. The yards of the houses stood back to back with a cobbled alley way between. Many people kept their wheelie bins in the alleyway these days as they had so many of them. Isobel couldn't see any that had fallen, probably someone staggering back from the pub, she thought. There was no-one in the alleyway and the woods to the side contained only darkness. Maybe it's the cat, thought Isobel. She pulled away from the window and closed the curtain. She suddenly felt very tired, she drank what was left of her milk, placed her book on the bedside table and turned off the light.

Isobel pulled the covers up around her. The bed was old, it creaked. She tossed and turned a few times until she got comfortable.

Eventually she became still, sleep wrapping her up. Her foot felt cold, she had pulled the covers up over it, she twisted and pulled it back in. The covers moved again and her foot and ankle were cold. Then she felt something warm, the grip of a hand on her ankle pressing down hard.

Chapter 23

James leaned back in his chair. Chewing on the end of his pencil he examined the ceiling tiles for inspiration. It was getting dark outside and the florescent tube light above his head in the incident room buzzed.

"I'm off." Evelyn said as she stood up and started putting on her coat.

"You're going home?" James asked and sat up straight in his chair.

"Yes. That is what most normal people do at some point." She wrapped her scarf around her and picked up her bag.

"But we're not normal people. We're CID"

"True on both counts but Lauren has dance practice." She started making her way to the door.

"Who's Lauren?"

"My daughter. I have mentioned her a few times and there's a picture of her on my desk."

"Oh yeh. I knew that." James glanced over at the framed photograph on Evelyn's desk. A smiling blond girl who looked as though she was on a camp site looked back at him and remembered he'd heard Evelyn mention her daughter before.

"I'll see you tomorrow." She called over her shoulder as she walked out of the room.

"yeh see you tomorrow" James mumbled.

James leaned forward and stared at the board in the incident room. He had put all of the five victims he believed were connected on there. His hope was that seeing all the victims details together would give him a eureka moment. There had not been one so far.

He didn't get it; no matter how hard he tried he just didn't get it. How could all these murders be committed by the same person? There was no pattern or any way of building a profile, and if they couldn't build a profile, how were they going to draw up a list of suspects? James downed his luke warm instant coffee and winced. He put the cup down on the desk and stood up to look at the map. There was a geographical profile at least. All of the victims were discovered in and around Hoddlesworth, also all of the victims were from Hoddlesworth, so maybe the killer didn't have a car? They relied on public transport or travelled on foot. James took a pen and started scribbling notes on the board. But then there was Levi? His body had been dumped at a different location, that would require transport and you could hardly transport a dead body on the bus. James scrubbed out the note he had written then threw the pen across the floor and paced around the room.

This room was in need of updating, he thought. He wondered around the now empty room, his shirt un-tucked, his tie loosened, his jacket and waistcoat now in a crumpled pile on the chair. The walls were still nicotine stained from the time when smoking in the work place was allowed, he looked closer, maybe they'd just been painted that colour? The carpet was worn and threadbare in places. There were spots of what looked like chewing gum that had been on the carpet so long the dirt had clung to them and turned them black.

James walked over to the window and stared into the night, his hands on his head. The yellow glow of the street lights, the darting white glare of the car headlights. All those people. Some on their way home, some already there, believing they were safe.

He kept replaying the words from the message, 'I'm not done yet.'

"So, tell me about these cases?" James turned around to see Oscar standing in the doorway; he didn't wait to be invited in but strolled around the room then began examining the incident board. He was crumpled like James but there was a sparkle in his James hadn't noticed before.

"Right, well" James dashed over to his desk and handed the case files to Oscar. He wasn't going to have another debate, he needed all the help he could get "We have five victims in total. All different, different MO, different …."

"Just start from the beginning" Oscar said. "Let's take each one individually."

"Ok" James began "So the first, we have Jenna Bishop, our youngest so far. She was strangled in her car, also her hair had been cut and her make-up removed. Again, no signs of forced entry, no signs of sexual assault, no DNA. She only had one earring. At first, we thought it was a straight forward crime of passions, angry ex-boyfriend, obsessed admirer but" James picked up his laptop and turned the screen to show Oscar the first blog post, "there was a note with a link to a web page, where we found this message."

"Second was Lucy Maxwell, 32 known prostitute and drug user, found dead in her flat. Cause of death was strangulation but she'd also received a blow to the head and was probably already unconscious when she died. There were no defensive wounds and no signs of forced entry at the flat so we presumed she knew her killer. There were no signs of sexual assault on the victim and no DNA evidence was found at the scene. The killer was most likely a customer, dealer or a pimp. However, there were two strange things about the scene, she was strangled with her own stockings; it was tied in a bow under her chin."

Oscar studied the picture in the case file. He remembered Lucy's face from the picture on the TV news. She barely looked like the same person in this photograph, but as he looked at it something came to him.

"I've seen this somewhere before, the Boston Strangler Alberto DeSalvo, killed women in their own homes, strangled them with tights or stocking then tied them in a bow under their chin. I thought you said there were no signs of sexual assault?"

"There weren't. She was wearing tights the stocking must have been taken from her draw. The second thing was the word 'strike' written on the mirror in lipstick."

"The third was Maureen Connelly, this is where we thought we had something because Maureen Connelly lived in the same block of flats as Lucy Maxwell, on the same floor even. Maureen was found at the bottom of a flight of stairs. At first neighbours thought she must have fallen but cause of death was established as a forceful blow to the head. 10/10 was written on her forehead in what we think was a bingo marker."

"You think it was a bingo marker?" Oscar asked. "Did she still have it with her when the body was discovered?"

"Erm, no why?"

"Every detail matters. Was Maureen Connolly a keen bingo player?"

"Yes. Her neighbours said that's where she was going when she was killed. Why? Look it's been a long day. Can you just tell me if I'm being stupid because..."?

"He's taking trophies. Did you find Lucy Maxwell's other stocking? Stockings come in pairs. One was tied around the throat where was the other? Levi Archer's cash box was taken because it was the only thing anyone would notice had gone missing from a cab."

"Contrary to what you might think, it had occurred to me that he might be taking trophies" said James "but I wanted a second opinion I guess."

"Tell me about the fourth?" said Oscar.

James continued "The fourth was Elaine Chase,46, school teacher. She was found at the school gates where she worked, single stab wound to the thigh, severed the femoral artery, also her left hand had been stamped on with some force. Every bone in her hand was broken. There was a note like a luggage tag tied to the railings that said A*. She didn't have her handbag with her."

"So, all female victims" Oscar said deep in thought, "could be someone with misogynistic tendencies. Maybe someone with a history of abuse, likely from the mother, or maybe he's never had much luck with women and has grown resentful. He wants to take his anger out where he can."

"We were pursuing that possibility" said James, "but then" he walked towards the incident board and pinned another picture to it. "Fourth victim" James continued "Levi Archer, 53, cab driver. He was found propped up at a picnic spot at Hoddlesworth Lake early this morning. His throat had been slit almost to the spinal cord and his neck was broken as if his head had been pulled back from behind. The word 'Goal' was carved into his side, most likely with the same knife that slit his throat although no murder weapon was found. No signs of sexual assault, no DNA." James paused and leaned on the back of his chair. "His cash box was missing, which at first made us think it could have been a robbery but the message on his side suggested otherwise."

Oscar drew in a deep breath "I don't think there can be any doubt we are dealing with a serial killer here, one who either has broad tastes or one who is deliberately trying to confuse us. I suggest we enforce a press blackout on this or risk creating mass hysteria. "

"Too late for that" James said "that blog has gone public. The killer has also started uploading the names and details of the other victims including pictures."

"Hmm. Is there any way we trace where this blog it updated from?" Asked Oscar

"I've looked in to that and apparently if it's being updated on 4G with a pay as you go phone with the GPS switched off, which apparently it is, then no, we can't trace it."

Oscar looked out of the window at the stream of moving lights in the darkness "People will want answers, assurances."

"What do you suggest we do?" James asked "I have racked my brains trying to figure this guy out!"

Oscar pulled up a chair and sat down. His eyelids felt less heavy than usual, the skin on his arms prickled, his brain pulsed "I suggest we order pizza and go over every detail of every case again. Even if it means we stay here all night."

Chapter 24

Oscar woke not to the drill of the alarm but to the crippling pain in his back. He reached out and stretched up, something clicked, "Ah that's better," he thought. There was a smell of stale garlic and grease in the air. James was leaning back in his chair. The pizza boxes were still on the desk mixed between the pieces of paper and case files. What time were they working until? He couldn't remember, they must have passed out about four or five am. They still hadn't gotten anywhere. This had to be the work of a serial killer. Oscar knew that much but he had never seen anything like this before, it was so random. How could they protect people if they didn't know who would be next?

Oscar rolled up a piece of paper and threw it at James, it hit him square on the forehead and he jumped awake. "Huh? What?"

"Wake up, its morning" Oscar said

"What? Oh god we were at this all night. What time is it?"

Oscar looked at his watch "Ten past seven" he said.

James stood up and stretched his legs "I need to freshen up. It smells like student digs in here" James shuffled the mouse on his desk and the screen came to life. He stared at it for a minute "We have a new message" he said.

Oscar walked over to James' desk and read what was on the screen "What is that supposed to mean? I will cross paths with the Lord if necessary."

"What does any of it mean" James said.

Evelyn came dashing down the corridor and marched through the door, still with her coat on and her coffee in her hand "Miller!" she cried "Oh Detective Superintendent, I wasn't expecting...."

"Detective Superintendent Black will be getting his hands dirty one final time and working with us on this case" James said.

"I don't remember actually agreeing to that "said Oscar trying to rub away the stiffness in his neck.

"You said it in your sleep." James said quickly. He turned to Evelyn, " So what are you in such a rush for?"

"There's been another" Evelyn said

"Where?" Oscar asked

"St George's church" Evelyn answered.

James and Oscar exchanged a look "I will cross paths with the Lord" James said

"What? "Evelyn asked her eyes darting between her two male colleagues.

James began putting his jacket on leaving his waistcoat on the chair "I will fill you in on the way." He made his way to the door and grabbed the coffee out of Evelyn's hand as he passed her "Mmmm thanks" he said with a smile "Let's go."

"But…" Evelyn protested but James was already half way down the corridor drinking her coffee.

"I take it he's always like this?" Oscar asked as he shrugged on his own coat.

"Always" Evelyn replied.

"Don't take it to heart; people are not always what they seem on the surface" he tapped her arm and walked towards the door.

"So I'm finding" Evelyn said.

Chapter 25

It was quiet. The orange early morning light had given way to and apple white glow painted across the gravestones and church spire created shadows beneath it. The pop-up white tent and yellow police tape were the only thing indicating this peace had been broken.

The car pulled up on the road, James turned and looked up at the church. It had been years since he had last been to church. He remember going with his grandmother; her talking to him about how sacred and special it was, how he must behave, must not mess about, must not raise his voice, he must remain as still and tranquil as possible. This church looked regal, especially in a small town like this. There was a stone wall that had turned greenish with moss over the years. In the centre were three small steps that lead up a wide gravel path to the church wall then turned a sharp right to up the main entrance at the bottom of the tower. James got out of the car, Oscar and Evelyn followed him, Oscar easing himself awkwardly out of the back seat and running his eyes along the shiny white car.

"They expecting DCIs to go undercover as drug dealers now?" he asked.

James continued walking down the path and pretended he hadn't heard. He imagined brides walking down that path excited for their big day and the life that lay ahead; he thought again to Sunday mornings with his grandmother. He pictured her gossiping with her friends delighting in what was possibly the first human contact of the week. He thought of funeral processions with bereaved relatives gathering together on this path for comfort. He remembered the day of his grandmother's funeral;

the church had felt serene and peaceful. Today that had been shattered. Today this church had been turned in to a cold, lonely place.

Half way up the main path another rocky rambling path lead off to the left and wound its way through the church yard between the gravestones and trees to a little gate in the stone wall. James followed the path until he saw the tent and addressed the officer "What do we have?" James asked.

"I'm not sure" the officer said "she had a handbag with her; it was placed on top of the body. We've managed to ID the victim as Isobel Montgomery-Smith, aged 56, lived in the local area. Take a look"

James stuck his head inside the tent, Isobel Montgomery-smith was lying on a gravestone. Her legs were straight out in front of her; ankles and knees touching, her arms had been crossed over her chest and her clothes were clean neat and tidy. Her grey hair had been brushed up into a neat tight bun and her eyes were closed.

Oscar appeared behind James closely followed by Evelyn, "Have we been able to establish a cause of death?" Oscar asked.

"Not yet" the officer said, "The post mortem will tell us more."

Oscar bent down to look closely at the victim's face "She's wearing a lot of make-up" he said.

"Lots of women wear too much make-up" Evelyn said.

"No this is like," he paused and thought for a moment "Have you ever seen a body in the chapel of rest?"

"I have" James said

"It looks kind of like that. Like someone had applied it after death, to make her seem more peaceful."

"So, she wasn't killed here?" Evelyn said.

"No" said Oscar "I think it's most likely she was killed elsewhere and her body was placed here and posed in this way."

"So first he takes make up off then he puts make up on?" James said "What is it with this guy?"

Oscar noticed something on the victims clothing, a stain across the abdomen, just peeping out beneath her folded arms. "Can I have some gloves please?" he asked. Oscar snapped on the latex gloves and carefully lifted the victim's cardigan then held his breath with what he saw, the abdomen was cut open, the wounds jagged and violent. The flesh had been pushed apart and the abdominal cavity was completely empty. "I suggest we start with her home address, see if there's anything there. Maybe the neighbours saw something." He put the cardigan back down where it had been.

James and Evelyn left the tent, Oscar looked at the victim for a moment then followed them back down the path towards the car "She's been ripped" Evelyn said.

"What?" James asked.

"Jack the Ripper disembowelled his victims. My guess is when you get a proper look at the body you'll find worse than that, especially if she was killed in a place where the killer knew there would be no interruptions."

"So, you're telling me we have a Jack the Ripper wannabe on our hands?" James asked.

"He wrote letters to the newspapers, taunted the police like our mystery blogger. Jack the Ripper only killed five people. It was the publicity and the way the murders were reported that made him famous."

"And the fact that he was never caught" said Oscar

"That too." Evelyn said

"Great" said James as he turned and walked back to the car. "We need to figure out where she was killed. He must have made a mess this time. There will be something, some shred of evidence we can link him to. There has to be."

As they approached the end of the path a woman wearing a pink fluffy dressing gown and trainers ran across the street towards them. She had large rollers still in her hair, her face was thick with make-up and one of her false eyelashes had fallen on to her cheek.

"What's going on? What's happened?" the woman wailed.

"Excuse me Miss could you step away please. This is a crime scene" said Evelyn.

"No! I will not just step away!" The woman was screeching and struggling to catch her breath. "I'm getting married here today, I can't have all this police tape in my photographs everything will be ruined."

James took the woman's hand "I'm very sorry he said, but the body of a murder victim has been found in the grounds of this church, we need to examine the crime scene very carefully."

The woman softened under his eyes, then she started to cry. "But it's my wedding day" she whimpered.

James placed his other hand on top of hers and just smiled sympathetically. The woman wiped her nose on the sleeve of her dressing down. "It's him isn't it?" she said "I saw the blog. Everyone's seen the blog. Everyone's talking about it. At first, I thought it wasn't real, that it was some sort of sick joke but this is him, isn't it? He's killed again!"

James stood up straight and let go of her hand "We are working on a list of suspects" he said officially.

The woman started to back away and looked around her "How do you know he's not still here, none of us are safe." Then she turned and ran back across the road.

Chapter 25

Press had gathered outside Isobel's house. The blog had gone public, images of all the victims, before and after they were killed, and the details of the latest victim including the address of the murder scene had been uploaded. Oscar, James, and Evelyn battled through the hoard of journalists, photographers, worried neighbours and general nosey parkers.

"Can we get a quote? How close are you to catching this killer?" shouted one journalist.

"Is it true you've had to get extra help from GMP?" shouted another.

"I heard it was a policeman" said a woman in the crowd. She walked right up to the three officers as they were trying to enter the house. Her face was drained and her eyes wide, she clutched her cardigan around her like a suit of armour "I heard it was a policeman and that's why you've not caught him. You're all covering up for each other! I've lived next door to Isobel for over twenty years and you couldn't ask to meet a nicer person. She wouldn't hurt a fly." The woman looked James straight in the eye "There's a sickness out there" she said "A sickness."

The crowd started jeering and shouting, louder and louder, pushing each other forward. Oscar felt himself being pushed forward, he knew he had to stay on his feet but the crowd kept pushing harder and shouting louder. Eventually Oscar made it inside the front door and took a deep breath as if he had just come up from underwater. Someone threw a bottle and it shattered on the wall by Evelyn's head. James pushed her inside as the uniformed officers tried to get the crowd under control his heart pounding and the sweat beginning to drip from his forehead.

James shut the front door behind them. They stood for a moment in the hallway in silence then Oscar walked towards the living room and opened the door. The smell was the same. No matter how many times he had been in these places he could never get used to it. They moved carefully across the room so as not to step on anything, the evidence needed to be preserved. The sun risked its luck and dared to peek through a gap in the heavy curtains revealing what had happened there. The room had been trashed. The furniture had been thrown around, tipped upside down; draws had been opened and emptied, the contents strewn across the floor. Ornaments and photo frames had been smashed and a bookcase had been pulled over scattering the books everywhere.

Oscar tried to remain professional. Above the fire place a message had been written on the mirror that read "Better than Bundy" with no question mark.

"So," James said to Evelyn "Looks like you were wrong. It's Ted Bundy our guy is a fan of not Jack the Ripper."

"Bundy was a sex attacker though," said Evelyn, "None of the victims so far have been sexually assaulted."

"Could it have been a burglary?" James asked as he walked around the room careful not to disturb anything "The victim just interrupted him?"

"And then the killer decided to paint her face, change her clothes, drive her to the church where she volunteered, lay her body out on a grave then send us a message about it" Evelyn said.

"She's right" said Oscar "This is staging. He's doing it deliberately to confuse us, to throw us off the scent of any real evident we may find here"

"Maybe whoever did this was just angry" Evelyn said "The other victims were killed in a controlled way. This violence all of this mess suggests this is someone who found some space and needed to lash out."

"Jenna Bishop wasn't killed in a controlled way" Oscar said. "Her hair was cut and her make-up rubbed off; I think this is more controlled than any of the others. He wants us to think he's angry. He's showing off. He wants us to know he's cleverer than we are. And maybe he wants us to stop him." The carpet was soaked in blood. In the fireplace were the remains of the clothing Isobel had been wearing at the time she was killed. Oscar bent down to get a closer look, he could make out a couple of pearl buttons. Everything burnt almost to dust to destroy any forensic evidence.

"How did you know the killer changed the victim's clothes? "Oscar asked Evelyn.

"Well it's obvious" she shrugged "Her clothes were clean. With nature of the injuries inflicted the clothes she had been wearing at the time of the attack would have been covered in blood. I always make it my business to pay attention to detail, sir."

Oscar stared at her for a minute "Good work inspector"

She smiled "Thank you sir"

They moved through to the dining room. The table, a beautiful dark antique oak, now resembled a slab in a butcher's shop. Blood had dripped down the cornicing and congealed in the grain. In the kitchen, knives and other instruments littered the floor; the cupboard doors were stained in stripes.

"There must be a finger print?" James asked the scene of crime officer.

"Not yet Gov" the officer said "Looks like he was wearing gloves"

"Keep looking" James said.

Oscar continued looking around the living room while James and Evelyn moved upstairs. The stairs were positioned between the living room and dining room; there were walls on either side and no windows at the top. Each step was covered in blood.

"This must have been her room" Evelyn said when they reached the landing.

"We need to see if anything's been taken, a trophy." Said James.

They made their way forward to the small box room. It was decorated in floral wallpaper with a number of religious pictures and ornaments. The bed was unmade and a lamp on the bedside table had been knocked over. A book lay open, page down on the floor. "She must have been in here" Evelyn said, "Or maybe she tried to hide up here, maybe thinking the killer was a burglar." She walked over to the bed and looked at something on the pillow. "There's blood on here, could be from a nose bleed."

"Or maybe the killer came up here, hit her on the head to knock her out, then dragged her downstairs" James said.

"It's possible" said Evelyn.

She walked back on to the landing and crouched in the bedroom doorway "The carpet here looks like it's been pulled back, that could be consistent with a heavy object being dragged across it." She stood up and walked back to the top of the stairs "It's escalating" she said "Our killer knows we're watching and is putting on a show."

James stared at her for a minute, something had appeared above her eyebrow, it moved down her face on to her eyelash, she winced and touched it. Then something else fell on her. They both looked up. What must have been the contents of Isobel's abdominal cavity were wrapped around the light fitting on the landing and the blood was dripping down on Evelyn's face.

Chapter 26

"Scene of Crime can finish up here, Evelyn, are you alright to stay?" James asked "I want you to see what else you can find that might give us some clues about this guy".

"I'm fine" she said. She was outside at the back of the house wiping her face with a tissue.

"It's just after Monday..."

Evelyn prickled "I told you it wasn't about the blood; it was that she was so young. I'm fine with this honestly. You go I can deal with things here." She shoved the tissue into her jacket pocket.

"Ok well you've got my number if you need me."

"Yes boss."

James turned and walked back inside the house to where Oscar was standing "I want you to come with me we can go over this new evidence" he said "see if we can find anything that tally up with the other victims, carry on where we left off last night. I suppose we better think about holding some sort of press conference to try to reassure people, somehow." Oscar nodded and said nothing his eyes still processing the scene.

They walked back through the house. Outside the crowd had grown in size and in volume. People shouted and threw things, took photographs. Others stood clutching small children to them, saying nothing at all but staring with pleading helpless eyes.

James and Oscar pushed their way through, eventually finding themselves back in the car.

James adjusted his tie nervously "Evelyn thinks this is escalating, that the killer is showing off." he said.

"I think she may be right" Oscar replied "The first few murders were quick; clean, blows to the head, strangulation. Maybe that was enough for him then but he got bored. He needs a bigger thrill now, more violence, more risk. He's taking his time, enjoying himself."

The car moved forward slowly as the crowd gathered around them. Cameras flashed. People banged on the windows and yelled. Someone threw an egg which hit the window on Oscar's side and smashed leaving bright yellow slime on the glass. James pumped the accelerator. The car growled and moved forward and people jumped out of the way. James drove on away, when they got to the end of the street he turned and headed back to the police station.

"That's not going to improve your public image" Oscar said.

James laughed, "Since when did you care about public image?" he said.

Oscar smiled to himself. Public image had always been the last thing on his mind; in fact, he almost went out of his way to give the public the worst image he could. He was rude and obtrusive to members of the press and public, much to the frustration of his bosses. Oscar thought back to one particular incident when a journalist was trying to infiltrate his crime scene, hanging around close to the police tape. Oscar was stood on the other side of the police tape drinking coffee and getting an update from the scene of crime officer. The journalist was shouting questions at him asking for a quote, so Oscar walked over. He said nothing but poured the contents of his coffee cup over the journalist's head. The journalist went away and stopped bothering them. However, the story he printed in the paper the following day was not favourable. Oscar's boss was not impressed. Oscar got results though and that's what mattered. He kept the bad guys off the streets for these people. Why should he have to be nice to them as well?

"I think Evelyn's right though, we need to hold a press conference, tell people something." James said.

"Seems Evelyn's right about a lot of things" said Oscar

"She is thinking logically keeping her head, which is more than I can say for me. Or you"

Oscar said nothing but shrugged his eyebrows in agreement and thought again of the journalist.

"I tell you what" James said "I really need to do something about this press conference so why don't you come over tonight? I'll do some food. We can go over some stuff then fresh environment away from the station. Pick up where we left off last night and try and make some sense of this."

"Thanks, but pot noodle doesn't really agree with me." Oscar said dismissively, then feeling guilty when thought over his own poor diet.

"I cook!" James protested

"Really? You cook?" Oscar was genuinely surprised. He had the polished pretty boy down for any practical skills.

"Yes. I'm a modern man." James pulled into the station car park.

"This I've got to see." He was intrigued, maybe he had misjudged James after all.

"Great. Be there at seven, I'll email you with the address."

Sunday 22nd September 2019

She reminded me of my Granny. Evil old cow. You're getting scared though now I can tell. I think I have a taste for this kind now. Perhaps I will find another.

Chapter 27

"Yes love. I know that's terrible. 45 minutes I waited for the bus on Thursday. It was that late by the time it came I'd missed my doctor's appointment. I tried to explain to the receptionist what had happened but she was having none of it, she just said there were no more appointments booked for that day and I'd have to come back again in a week. A week! I could be dead by then, I said, but she wasn't bothered, just that was the earliest they could fit me in." Elizabeth Robertson was on the phone to her sister Edith. Elizabeth lived alone in her first-floor warden controlled flat but spoke to Edith on the phone every other day. They would meet up every Tuesday and go in to town, do some shopping round the market then go for lunch in a little café; always the same café, always the same lunch; egg mayonnaise sandwich for Edith, ham salad sandwich for Elizabeth and a pot of tea for two. They had been doing this every Tuesday since they both retired 15 years ago, Elizabeth thought it was important to get out of the house and keep in a routine when she retired. That was why she also volunteered in a charity shop two days a week.

"Yes, so I'll see you tomorrow, I'll meet you in the precinct at half past ten, providing the bus is on time that is. No I hadn't hear about Betty...what did he?. He never?....well I had heard people saying..." The intercom buzzed. "Just a minute love there's someone at the door. Yes, I'll ring you back in a bit." Elizabeth hung up the phone and went to answer the door.

C

"Police are calling him the West Pennies Killer, the man responsible for a string of murders across the Hoddlesworth area. The victims have varied in age, race and gender but police are certain they are all connected after a series of blogs appeared giving details of the victims and taunting the police. Detective Chief Inspector James Miller had this to say "We are currently investigating a string of murders across the region that we believe are the work of one perpetrator. We are following a number of leads but would like to stress that there is no need for panic or alarm. Thank you." We have been informed that a full press conference will be held tomorrow afternoon where police will appeal for further information. In the meantime, it is advised the public remain vigilant and inform the police of anyone they see acting suspiciously. "

Craig Underwood shovelled another forkful of instant mash potato into his mouth, his eyes fixed on the tea time news. He was aware the food on the tray balanced on his knee was getting cold. His wife emerged at the bottom of the stairs dressed in tracksuit bottoms and a training t-shirt with the slogan "Suck it up Princess" written in neon pink italics across the front. She sat in the arm chair on the opposite side of the room and began putting her trainers on, "You not finished that yet love? It'll be cold."

"I was watching the news" said Craig "There's a serial killer on the loose apparently."

"Yes, it's all over the papers. The woman on the checkout in Tesco was talking to me about it, said she won't get the bus home any more, makes her husband come out and pick her up." She bent down to examine her laces again. "Load of rubbish if you ask me" she mumbled.

"Police are saying to be vigilant"

She smiled "Well I shall be sure to be extra vigilant on my way home from step aerobics. I'll see you when I get back." She picked up her bag and gave Craig a brief kiss. He flinched but she didn't notice and headed for the front door.

"I won't be in" Craig said "When you get back. I'm playing badminton at seven with Martin and we said we might go for a drink afterwards."

"Martin? From work I thought you didn't like him, you said he was a backwards idiot."

"Well maybe I've seen another side to him."

"It's no good playing badminton then re-consuming your calories in the pub afterwards. I'll be looking slim on the beach in Spain even if you won't."

Craig gagged on his mash potato.

Craig looked back down at his mash potato admonished "I'm just trying to be sociable" he said.

"Yes, well, it's all well and good being sociable but there's things need doing here. You said you were going to clear out that garage."

"I'll do it this weekend."

"You said that last weekend. I'll do it myself."

"No!" said Craig "I'll do it!"

His wife stood up straight and adjusted the hem of her t-shirt, "Right, well, see that you do. I'm off."

She left. Craig continued to eat his mash and stare at the TV screen.

Chapter 29

James' flat was exactly as Oscar had imagined. It was on the top floor of a modern purpose-built apartment building. On the outside it was all white render with clean lines and chrome accessories at odds with the grey weathered and worn buildings that filled the rest of the town. Inside it was open plan; neutral, sterile like an operating theatre. Contrary though to Oscar's expectations James had a lot of stuff around the place - a lot of stuff. He had books, DVDs, even CDs but they were all still in boxes. Many had overflowed on to the floor where he had been rummaging through them trying to find something in particular; then the stuff had stayed on the floor. It was like he had bought the flat for the person he wanted to be. The cool calm professional was always beaten down by the excitable hopeful child. Instead of a fire place there was a huge flat screen TV occupying the main wall and there were some dumbbells and other fitness equipment, some of it still in several pieces, on the floor beneath it. At the end of the room were a set of glass bi-folding doors that led to a small balcony beyond. On the wall was a pair of boxing gloves in a glass case with an autograph that Oscar couldn't make out.

"You a big boxing fan?" he asked

"What?" James said looking up from concentrating very hard on a jar of dried herbs, "Oh no not really, I saw them on eBay just after I bought this place, I thought they'd look cool on the wall."

"Hmmm" Oscar said and made a face involuntarily, "Yeh, they look erm, good,"

The smells coming from the kitchen reminded Oscar of an Italian restaurant and there was a Jamie Oliver cook book propped open on the counter.

"I brought wine "Oscar said handing over the bottle as James stirred the thick red sauce in the pan.

"Oh great." He looked at the label and nodded like he wanted to look like he knew what he was taking about "Take a seat" he said directing Oscar to the black leather L shaped sofa.

"You might want to let that breathe for a bit" Oscar said nodding towards the wine.

"Oh, right yeh" said James looking for a corkscrew.

Oscar stood up and looked out across the balcony "Nice place."

"It's alright I guess, feels a bit cold, you know" James poured one glass of wine then went to pour another.

"Oh no, not for me" Oscar said as he tried to find one of his excuses "I'm driving, I can't have another night like last night, I need my bed. Water is fine"

"Oh right, yeh, of course" James said. "He'd heard," Oscar thought.

James filled two glasses, one with wine, one with water then walked across the room and handed the one filled with water to Oscar "I'm not too sure I'm cut out for this minimalist stuff." James said "I think it was designed for someone tidier than me." James drank a gulp of wine and winced.

Oscar looked down at a cardboard box filled with old football magazines "I think you might be right there," he said.

Something sizzled loudly and James ran back to the kitchen. There was a period of frantic stirring, the opening and closing of cupboard doors, the clattering of plates and cutlery before James said "Dinner is served!" He carried two plates over to the round glass table, Oscar sat down as James proudly placed in front of him a plate of spaghetti and meatballs in a tomato sauce.

"Looks great" said Oscar, "This you're signature dish?" James picked up a forkful of spaghetti. "Well, this and chicken stir-fry, they're about the only thing I can make" he said with a smile.

The orange sky turned to blackness as they ate. The clattering of forks, the scratching of plates almost made the situation seem normal. Oscar couldn't remember the last time he'd sat at a table instead of balancing a tray on his knee. He took another glance around at James' very definite bachelor pad and it occurred to him that maybe James couldn't either.

James leaned back in his chair as he finished eating "So what happened?" he asked.

"What do you mean?" Oscar replied.

"You were the number one detective on the force; I knew your name as soon as I joined. Then all of a sudden you turned in to some cynical pen pusher. Something must have happened."

"Well it didn't."

"It must have. You don't just stop loving the job just like that."

Oscar looked down at the stem of his glass "Time happened, too many innocent people losing their lives, too many bad guys getting away with it." He could see Carrie's face.

"It doesn't mean you stop trying."

"Sometimes there's nothing left to try for."

There was a long pause in the conversation until James said, "You married?"

"I was. Not now." Oscar said briskly "What about you? It doesn't look like there's much of a feminine touch to this place."

"No" James laughed "My mother comes around and tries to tidy up now and again but apart from that not at all. I like to shop around."

"It's easy to say that when you're young, gets lonely when you get to my age."

"Is that why you're divorced? Too much shopping around?"

Oscar took a sip of his water and gulped it down hard as if he was hoping it would make it have an effect "I didn't say I was divorced" he said quietly, "The job was my mistress. Too many late nights, too many weekends not at home."

"She is a demanding mistress indeed. I thought you said you weren't married anymore?"

"No." Oscar paused. "She died, cancer, ten years ago now."

"I'm sorry." James said.

"It's ok." Said Oscar automatically. He carried on staring at the stem of his glass for a few moments then spoke again, "Except it's not ok. I retire in six months. We had so much planned we were going to sell the house and buy a narrow boat, travel around Britain by canal. Moor up at pub overnight then set off again in the morning and see where the water took us." He decided not to mention that The Chief wanted him gone even sooner.

"Really? You don't seem like the outdoors type" James laughed kindly

Oscar laughed too "No, well I'm not. It was more Marie's idea really and I felt it was fair that she should get to do what she wanted. Like I said I spent too much time at work. I didn't even notice she was ill until, well, until it was too difficult for her to hide it anymore, until it was too late to make amends. Three weeks, three weeks after she told me she was gone." He paused. "It was just me alone in that big house with only a bottle of whiskey for company." He thought about The Chief's offer.

James nodded, he knew what it was like to want to block out reality.

"She tried to tell me" Oscar said "She tried a few times, but I was always too busy to listen."

"Sometimes we need to listen to what people are trying to tell us. It's sad that often we don't realise what a difference it could have made until it's too late."

Oscar went silent and stared in to the middle distance "Have you got copies of those blog posts?"

"They're in the case file." James got up and brought the files to the table Oscar looked through them frantically. "What?" James asked.

"Some of the victims were killed at home, some were moved. Some are similar to the killing of Ted Bundy some the Boston strangler Alberto DeSalvo"

"Some were strangled, some were stabbed."

"Look, the first one posted and the third one spell 'your' meaning you are is spelt wrong, the second one posted after Isobel's death is spelt 'you're' as in the correct way." Oscar felt a surge of heat rush over his skin. He could hear his blood pumping like a derelict car engine that had suddenly spurted back to life.

"So, a lot of people get that mixed up?" James waved his had dismissively and took another drink.

"No" Oscar was transfixed with the pieces of paper in his hands, "most people either don't understand it or they're stubborn about getting it right. They don't get it wrong on some occasions and then right on others." He turned to James who was now also staring at the words on the pages, "I think we are dealing with two different people."

Chapter 30

After Oscar left James took out the case files and spread them across the table. He took out a pad of paper and a pen and made two columns. He wrote the words 'Killer One' at the top of one column and 'Killer Two' at the top of the other. Then he started working through the list of victims and assigning them to each killer. Lucy Maxwell and Maureen Connolly, they were both killed by a blow to the head; he put them under killer one. Then there was Levi Archer and Isobel Montgomery-Smith. Their deaths were more violent, they were both killed in knife attacks. He put them under killer two. Then there was Elaine Chase, she had been stabbed but her death had been quick, and Jenna Bishop, no knife wounds but still a high level of violence. James started chewing on the end of the pen in his hand, how did this work? Did one take the lead on one killing and the other on the next? It explained why the victims were so varied but it still didn't make sense. He returned to his faithful coffee machine.

Hours passed and the dirty coffee cups were stacked in a pile on the floor next to the sofa. James leaned back and creaked his neck. Through the balcony doors he could see the sun beginning to rise above the outlined of the hills. He had been going through the victims all night, swapping them back and forth from one column to another but he still couldn't make any sense of it. He yawned and looked at his watch; he had to start sleeping better soon.

James felt his eyes close, they felt so heavy it was as if he was powerless to stop them. Just for minute he thought. He felt his muscles relax, the swirling of his mind going slower and slower, then the phone rang. The sound jolted him awake; he searched though the piles of paper and eventually found his phone. He saw Evelyn's name flashing up on the screen. He knew what she was going to say before he answered.

Chapter 31

The Aston Martin growled as Oscar changed gear. He was driving too fast. Maybe he should have used sirens but he'd not done that for years. It was still early and the roads were quiet. He pressed his foot down on the accelerator further and the engine growled deeper.

He didn't know much about this murder. He didn't want to know until he arrived at the scene. His foot eased up and his stomach tightened. Up until this week It had been twenty years since he'd last set foot in a crime scene. He had taken to getting the rest of his team to do that for him and report back, but yesterday he felt alive, knowing there must be something there, something that would lead to the killer. This killer was smart and it was no good being smart if no-one knew who you were. Oscar thought about that day again, twenty years ago. The heat, the smell. He thought about the days afterwards too, so many days waking up with a taste of failure in his mouth, downing a double whiskey first thing to wash it away. Turning up at the station believing he was fine, he brushed his teeth, he used mouth wash, hoping no-one would notice. Except they did notice, when he fell over climbing the stairs, when he started arguments if someone bumped in to him in the canteen, when he threw up whilst interviewing a suspect, of course they noticed. Everybody noticed.

Today was different, he was different. Stone cold sober and alive again. The outcome would be different too, Oscar was going to catch these guys if it was the last thing he did.

Chapter 32

It was early, a thin mist lingered as did the scents of the night before. Smell of fried onions, spices, sauces and grease from the takeaways and restaurants in the adjoining street hung in the air like a mosquito net.

James sat on a bench and put his head in his hands. Oscar sat down next to him.

"Pull yourself together lad" Oscar said "You're supposed to be leading this investigation."

James looked away "Well maybe someone else would be better leading it" he said.

Oscar sighed and started to walk back inside "I knew it. I've seen loads like you over the years. Only interested in the perks, the social status, the pension. I had started to think I was wrong about you but I guess not. You just go running back to your safe little existence as soon as things get tough. You're right; you're not up to this. Step down before any more innocent people get killed."

James stood up abruptly, "I don't care about my pension plan, or throwing my badge around so I can get cheap drinks after hours, this job is my life! I am the job!"

Oscar stopped walking and turned around "Yeh? Well prove it then. Get back in there and let's try and figure out what we are dealing with here."

James followed Oscar back up the stairs to the first floor flat. Evelyn was crouched down beside the body examining it closely. It was still on the living room floor where the warden had found it, a stocking wrapped around the victim's neck and tied in a bow.

James took a deep breath "So we have Elizabeth Robertson, 78, widowed, lived alone. Initial inspection would indicate cause of death to be strangulation but it would also appear the victim suffered a blunt force trauma to the head." The flat was clean, neat tidy, everything was where it should be in complete contrast to the scene at Isobel Montgomery-Smith's house. James felt more confused than ever.

"Her wedding ring's missing" Evelyn said "She has a very pronounced indent on the fourth finger of her left hand which suggests she has been wearing a ring on that finger for some time but now it's gone."

"That's his trophy for this one" said Oscar. "What trophy was taken, from Isobel Montgomery-Smith?"

"We haven't been able to establish that" Evelyn said, "It doesn't look like it's anything obvious."

"She's also been strangled with tights' that have been tied in a bow and killed in her own home, just like Lucy Maxwell" Evelyn continued.

"Do we have a message anywhere at the scene?" asked James

"No but there has been another update on the blog" Evelyn handed James the tablet and he read the message.

Tuesday 24th September 2019

So sweet so trusting, she let me right in just like Granny. I wonder who will be next?

"The Boston Strangler, again" James said "Do these guys have some trading sticker serial killer obsession? Jack the Ripper, Ted Bundy and the Boston Strangler?"

"It might explain why the murders are all so different" said Oscar "They're copycats, but instead of coping one killer they're copying them all."

"What's going on?" Evelyn asked "What do you mean *they?*"

"We came up with a theory, or rather Oscar did, that we are not just dealing with one killer but two. That's why the murders vary so much."

"Oh, I see" said Evelyn "And when did you arrive at this theory? Maybe it would be a good idea to let the rest of the team in on it."

"I was going to, we only thought of it last night."

"Really? Last night?"

"Oscar came around, I wanted to pick his brain."

Evelyn crossed her arms over her chest.

"Maybe they are working as some sort of tag team" said Oscar, "One taking the lead on one murder then the other on the next. That's why some are violent and some are quick."

Evelyn uncrossed her arms and placed her hands in her back pockets and shrugged "Well at least we have some sort of theory, I suppose."

"I'll take any leads we can get on this one" James said "We need to get back to the station. The press conference is scheduled for 10:30 this morning."

"Good" Evelyn said "Panic is setting in and I don't just mean from the public. I'm sitting in on this press conference with you whether you like it or not."

Chapter 33

Chairs shuffled, voices mumbled, plastic coffee cups cracked then swished as they descended into the bin. James stood with Evelyn peering out from behind the curtain. The room beyond was small and it seemed to get smaller every second.

"I don't know what to tell them." He said "They want answers and I don't have any"

"You're letting your bravado slip Detective Chief Inspector" Evelyn smiled and her face softened.

James smiled back "I think it's been on the slide for a while now. This case has got me baffled; I don't see how we have a hope in hell of catching these guys. They seem to pick any victim any location, anyone of these people could be next." He nodded towards the crowd.

"But they don't need to know that do they? You go out there and you put on that swagger, give them that smile, that arrogance"

James laughed a little "Arrogance?" he said.

"Come on you know it's there. There are a lot of people, particularly women, who find that appealing"

"Is that right?"

"I'm not one of them of course" she smiled "now go out there and razzle dazzle them. Oh, and maybe you shouldn't say anything about this two-killer theory, not yet."

James nodded, "Where's Black?"

Evelyn rolled her eyes, "This is not his case it's yours. I'll be out there with you and I've thrown a grieving relative in for good measure."

"What relative?"

"Edith Jones, Elizabeth Robertson's sister. A few tears should help jog someone's memory."

They walked through the curtains. There was a long table on a slightly raised platform with chairs and a microphone and a glass of water set at each one of them. Edith was helped to her seat by a police liaison officer. She looked frail, a mere wisp of a thing. Her sister had not been sturdy by any means but somehow James got the impression she had been a force to be reckoned with. Edith seemed like a small bird that might fall out of the sky at any moment; her head was bowed like she no longer had the strength to stand up straight. Had she always been like that, James thought, or had her sister's death taken away some of her life too?

Evelyn and James took their seats. James was in the middle next to Edith with Evelyn to his left. Cameras snapped and questions fought over each other as they sat down. James raised his hand for silence "There will be time for questions later, first I would like to address the situation. As you are no doubt aware a public blog has surfaced which has been linked to a number of recent murders in the area. We have reason to believe that this is not a hoax and the person responsible for this blog is our killer. We are pursuing a number of leads at present and feel very certain that the perpetrator will be apprehended in the very near future. In the meantime, we ask the general public to be vigilant and report any information they feel may be relevant to our incident room. We believe this individual to be extremely dangerous. If you have any reason to believe you may know who this person is, or if you are protecting anyone please contact us immediately. To my right is Mrs...."

"Miss" Edith said.

"Miss Edith Jones. Sadly, her sister Elizabeth was the most recent victim of this vicious killer. Miss Jones, I believe you have a statement prepared?"

"Yes. Elizabeth and I were born only 11 months apart, many people used to mistake us for twins. We did everything together growing up and these past 15 years, since Elizabeth lost her dear husband John, we had really become each other's other half. I really do feel like half of me has gone today. This man has not just taken away one life he has taken two. If you are watching this and have any shred of conscience please hand yourself in and make this stop before any more lives are ruined. Thank you."

"Thank you, Miss Jones," James said "Any questions?"

"DCI Miller how do you intend to reassure the public?" A journalist asked.

"We would like to remind the public that to become the victim of any violent crime committed by a stranger is a very rare occurrence. There is no need for panic."

"Do you have any suspects?" Another journalist asked.

James wavered.

"We are not at liberty to divulge that information at this stage" Evelyn interrupted "However we can say that we are pursuing a number of lines of enquiry"

A buzz descended on the room, everyone began talking among themselves and checking their phones and laptops.

"What's going on?" James whispered to Evelyn.

"My guess is, our blogger has sent another update." She said.

Tuesday 24th September 2019

You think you're so clever, it was pretty obvious really. I like clever people though. I've got a good one lined up next.

Chapter 34

Oscar crossed the road at the pelican crossing. A good citizen. The sky was darkening and the street lights were beginning to glow. He walked past the church. He needed to think. He needed caffeine. He turned sharply to his left and through the swinging plastic doors into the shopping centre. Most people were leaving but he knew this place would still be open, for him anyway. He waited at the door to be seated as the sign instructed. A happy young couple were eyeing up rings in the window of the jewellers next door. Just engaged? He thought, or maybe he was about to propose and looking for ideas? Or maybe this was a first date that was going really well? He couldn't be sure. He was sure though that they were happy, excited for the future. Could they be next? He couldn't be sure of that.

The waitress, Sally, recognised him from across the counter; she waved him in and gestured towards his usual table. The heavy wooden chair screeched across the cream tiled floor. Oscar sat down. This was his favourite place to sit. The café's end wall was curved glass. He liked to sit just on the edge of it with his back against the wall, a great position to see everything that was going on in the outside world and inside the café, without looking like a spy and hidden enough so that no-one would spy on you.

Oscar liked this place. Slightly up on the traditionally copper greasy spoon but not some American chain pretending to be Italian. He had been coming here since it opened three years ago. He came here when he needed a place of sanctuary and didn't want to be tempted by the pub. The owners had made a vain attempt to bring a slice of European café culture to this northern town by placing a few tables outside in the small courtyard that formed the entrance to the shopping centre. Currently they were occupied by a couple of desperate smokers pitifully shivering over their cappuccinos and debating whether or not it was time to pull the hoods up on their coats.

"Hiya Oscar, will it be the usual?" Sally asked.

"You know me too well" Oscar said "Black coffee please, Sally"

"Right with you" Sally headed off back to the counter.

Oscar looked out of the window at the gaggle of people. There were the organised ones who had already started their Christmas shopping, the harassed ones who were heading home from work, the lonely ones who spent the day wondering around town hoping to find someone to talk to, the excited ones just heading into town for a night on the tiles. Anyone of them could be next.

"Your black coffee sir" Oscar looked up briefly. A gangly, ginger haired young waiter placed the perfectly white cup with its black steaming contents and complimentary napkin in front of Oscar.

"Thank you" Oscar muttered while still staring out of the window. The waiter began to straighten the chairs at the adjoining tables.

"You're right you know" the waiter said. Oscar wasn't really listening and thinking this was an attempt to make small talk pretended he hadn't heard. "Well, you're right and you're wrong."

"What, sorry?" Oscar asked.

The waiter nudged the table with one of the chairs and the coffee in the cup sloshed over the sides and on to the table. Oscar reached over for the napkin and began to unfold it.

"You're right that there are two of them but you're wrong about them being a team" the waiter said "It's a competition."

Oscar looked over in his direction. The waiter smiled. Just then there was a scream outside in the street. Some teenagers in fancy dress that had caught the Halloween bug early and jumped out on a woman and scared here when Oscar looked back into the café the youth had gone. Then something else caught his eye, there was something written on the napkin he was holding, an address. He rushed over to Sally who was drying cups behind the counter.

"Where's that guy gone? How long has he worked here? What do you know about him?"

"What guy?" Sally asked.

"That guy! A young lad a bit gangly, ginger hair"

Sally looked puzzled and shook her head "I'm sorry Oscar I don't know who you mean. I don't think we have anyone like that working here."

Chapter 35

Oscar entered the station through the side entrance; he didn't want to bump in to anyone. He pushed through several sets of double doors and made his way down to the basement, that's where the evidence room was. He knew exactly where he was going, he had been over the evidence from this case many times. He remembered the day he was finally convinced to shelve this case. He remembered every step he took down to that basement, the box of evidence in his arms. It didn't seem like much. It had been five years and still all the evidence they had gathered managed to fit inside one box. He had insisted on taking everything down in the incident room himself. He unpinned every drawing pin, folded everything neatly and placed it inside the box. He could see Carrie's face the whole time, sitting there on the stairs in her school uniform, innocent and bewildered. He knew what she would say if she could see him now, that he had let her down. As he had placed the box on the shelf he promised himself that he would come back for it one day and today was that day.

The day he put it down here he had promptly left the station and gone home to get blind drunk. That was the first time. The first time he drank to oblivion, drank to forget, drank not to feel. It was to be the first of many.

He carried the box upstairs to the incident room. These murders had started the day the paper had published the 20th Anniversary appeal for information about the Worthingtons' murders. There may be something in that box, some kind of clue. As he passed the main entrance he saw one of the cleaners arriving for work. A man, he assumed must be her husband had escorted her to the front door. Oscar had never seen him do that before. People were scared. They were staring to panic.

Oscar walked into the incident room and started going through the box. He knew there was something else he needed to do. He sat down at his desk and sent an email.

Chapter 36

Geoff Hudson was a regular guy; in fact, you'd probably be hard pushed to find a more regular guy than Geoff. He was a plumber and made a decent living. He lived with his wife, their two daughters and their dog, Brandy, in a very regular three bedroom semidetached house. On Mondays Geoff went to the pub quiz with his two best friends from school, Andy and Bob. They had been friends for over 30 years and Monday nights was their time. 'Indestructible' was their quiz team name. They would drink beer, eat crisps, talk about football, cars, work, all very regular.

When the quiz had finished and Geoff had said goodnight to Andy and Bob he would begin his walk home. The pub wasn't far from his house, particularly if you took the short cut. There was a school just around the corner from the pub and the playing fields ran right up to the fence of Geoff's back garden. There was a public footpath that ran along the side of the fields and came out right on Geoff's street. Geoff always warned his wife and daughter not to use the footpath especially after dark as there were no street lights and you never knew who might be creeping up behind you. He always told them to go the long way around where it was well lit and safe. The problem with the long way around though, was, well, that it was a very long way around, and Geoff was a man; a big strong slightly overweight man currently fortified by three pints of larger. He would take the short cut. He would be fine.

Geoff turned the corner on to the footpath. The darkness closed in around him, squeezing him tight. He picked up the pace a little. One side of the path was lined with a crumbling red brick wall that used to enclose the grounds of the local hospital. It had been used to treat TB patients at the turn of the last century but had long since been closed down and turned in to a housing development. The wall had been kept as an interesting feature to bump the house prices up. Kids in the neighbourhood always said the grounds were haunted. They said the Grey Lady still walked the ground at night calling out for her lost lover. An owl hooted. Geoff picked up the pace a little more.

It was a clear night. Clear and still with barely a breeze. The other side of the path was lined with trees, many had already lost their leaves and they crumbled under Geoff's feet. The few that remained did their best to block out the light from the moon. Geoff heard a noise, soft, fast. Too small and quick to be human, he thought, do squirrels come out at night? A Cat then? Geoff picked up the pace a little more again; he was getting out of breath now. About half way down the path there was a bend, Geoff knew when he rounded that it was a straight line to the end. He would be able to see the glow of the street lights, the street lights on his street. He would be almost home. When he got there he would open his front door and the house would be warm inside. He would take of his shoes, feel the carpet soft beneath his feet, he would go upstairs and slip into bed beside his wife, wrap the warm duvet around him and fall in to a deep sleep.

He turned the bend anticipating the relief. He felt something soft and cold brush against his forehead. He jumped back, his heartbeat quickened, his mouth went dry. There in his eye line framed by the faint traces of moonlight was a human foot.

Monday 30th September 2019

So clever, so pretty so perfect. Long dark hair parted down the middle, perfect. So helpful too, with my flat tyre. Silly girl. Now over to you.

Chapter 37

"Vanessa Marsden, 20, university student. We found a driving license on her but no student card, that could have been taken as the trophy. She grew up in Hoddlesworth and had come home for a few days to visit her parents. They dropped her off at the train station a week ago believing she would be on the 11:30 am train back to University in Durham. When they didn't hear from her they just assumed she was back at uni having fun with her mates. Her body was discovered about 11:30 last night by a passer-by." Evelyn said.

The light was dim. The trees were black and stark next to the grey sky.

"Cause of death was a blow to the head not hanging." Evelyn continued "She's been dead a while I'd say. Kept somewhere then put and posed in this way."

"Bundy did that didn't he?" James asked "Went back and visited the corpses of his victims?"

"He did. Looks like you've been reading some books Detective Chief Inspector."

A magpie squawked, a bus rolled past on the main road in the distance.

"Isobel Montgomery-Smith. She was killed at home then her body was moved and staged, so was Levi Archer but Elizabeth Robertson and Lucy Maxwell were killed in their own homes and the bodies were left at the scene. I think Oscar maybe on to something" James said "If our killer is copycatting different serial killers it could explain why the MO keeps changing"

Evelyn just nodded "What does this mean for our investigation?" she asked.

"It means we're going to have a lot more difficulty creating a profile, and even more difficulty narrowing down suspects."

James rubbed his hands through his hair and looked down at the body.

"It doesn't mean it can't be done." Evelyn said "If we catch these killers it'll make us the greatest detectives in history"

"Or the biggest failures, if this carries on and more people die. I need to get back to the station, I want you to stay here and keep an eye on these clowns." He pointed to the gaggle of journalist's photographers and TV crews that had emerged at the end of the passageway "Make sure none of them get too close, we can't afford to have whatever shreds of evidence that may be here contaminated, and only tell them what they need to know."

"Do we know anything we can tell them?"

"No, but like you said they don't need to know that. Where's the guy who found her?"

"Over there, the victim's mother's been hanging around too. You might want to speak to her. I've tried to get her to go home but she won't hear of it."

Geoff was sat in the back of a police van with a red blanket wrapped around him staring at the floor. He looked up when he saw James approaching "This is meant to help with the shock" Geoff said gesturing to the blanket "Not sure how exactly."

James hopped up on to the back of the van Evelyn hovered outside "I'm not sure either" James said "They send me on all these first aid courses but I'm terrible for not paying attention. Are you ok to answer a few questions?"

Geoff nodded.

"Can you just tell me exactly what happened last night? What you saw?"

"I was walking back from the pub, we'd been to the quiz. I only live there." Geoff pointed over the field. "I don't always go this way, I know it's dark and anyone could be lurking in the bushes, that's what I'm always telling my daughter anyway, but really it's a safe area this and I never thought anything would actually happen so a took the short cut."

"And what time was this?"

"About 11, maybe just after. I was walking pretty quickly, I wanted to get home, it was cold. You forget how dark it gets when there aren't any street lights." He tried to laugh but it came out as more of a sob "It touched me. That's how I knew. I couldn't see it in the dark, but, I felt it, I walked right in to it, her foot. Her foot it touched my head!" Geoff was staring to shake and wrapped the blanket around himself tightly.

"It's ok sir; did you see anyone else or hear anything, a car maybe?"

"No, not a soul. There was no one. It was so dark though, like I said there are no street lights, you take them for granted, it gets so dark" Geoff stared off towards the trees and started shaking his head frantically "No, no, no, there was no-one. There was no-one!"

"Ok that's all for now." James nodded towards the medical officers to take over.

He jumped down from the van. You've got the mother to deal with now" Evelyn said.

James took a deep breath and kept walking. Close to the police tape by the wall there was a woman standing in her dressing gown and slippers clutching a battered old teddy bear. James ducked under the tape "Mrs Marsden?" he asked, the woman nodded. "Why don't you let one of our officers take you home? Put some warmer clothes on then we will be round to take a statement?"

Mrs Marsden shook her head "I want to be here" she said her eyes fixed on the little white tent in the distance.

"I really would recommend you go home Mrs Marsden" James said.

"Are you sure? Are you sure it's her?" she asked. James looked to Evelyn but she said nothing.

"We will need you to make a formal identification but we are fairly certain we have found the body of your daughter Vanessa, she had her driving licence on her."

"She was such a sweet girl, so clever." Mrs Marsden stroked the teddy bear in her hands.

James put his hand on her elbow and managed to gently turn her away. He ushered her down to where the family liaison officer was waiting "I'm very saw for your loss Mrs Marsden" James said.

"You'll get him, won't you?" She asked.

James looked at her unable to say anything. The family liaison office lead her away to the waiting car.

James turned on his heel and walked back towards Evelyn "Well, you were a big help there" he said.

"I thought you didn't need me anymore, where's your new partner?"

"Oh, for goodness sake stop being so childish. I've enough to deal with without you throwing your toys out of the pram. I had to get extra help we weren't exactly getting very far on our own."

"We're still not getting very far. We still have no suspects."

"Maybe not, but we are closer than we were and we'll get closer still if we stick together and work as a team instead of glory hunting. There are people's lives at stake here, not just you career. I'll see you back at the station." James turned and marched back to his car.

Chapter 38

James swung through the Police Station doors. The lobby had been rejuvenated a lot more recently than the incident room; this was the side the public saw. Everything was either white or glass, clean, transparent. James walked through the glass double doors across the white glossy tiled floor to the front desk with its glass counter top.

Julie on the front desk smiled at him like she was a receptionist in a hotel and he was paying customer there for an exciting weekend.

"If any reporters come in here you tell them we have no comments to make and any further updates will be issued by our press office."

"Will do" Julie said "There is someone else who wanted to speak to you" Julie pointed with a pen to the corner of the lobby area where a cylinder made of glass blocks formed a feature on the outside of the building and a small circular waiting area inside the reception. Sitting one of the chairs was a women James recognised. She was small, skinny, with bleached blond hair that showed her dark roots, smudged make-up around her faded blue eyes but still with a bright smile. She was dressed in a tight red mini dress, high heeled boots and a faux fur coat.

"Amelia" James said with a smile, "Long time no see."

"Well I was passing by so I thought I'd look you up." Amelia leaned back against the glass tiles and smiled.

"Passing by? You mean you spent a night in the cells?"

"Not my fault, everyone's got to earn a living and I don't see enough of you anymore."

"Yeh well I transferred from vice a while back."

"Shame. I hear you're dealing with murders now?"

James nodded "Amongst other things."

Amelia stood up and leaned closer to James as if she was about to tell him a juicy secret "There's a serial killer on the loose, that's what they said on the news anyway."

James leaned in closer "Well, people like to have a crisis, don't read too much into it."

"I'm worried. All the girls are."

"Well there is no need."

"I think there is a need. We working girls are serial killer fodder, have been for centuries. We're the less dead; people don't miss us like they miss respectable citizens."

"I'm not going to pretend that there are no risks associated with your occupation but you have no reason to believe that you are at any more risk from a serial killer right now than anybody else."

"Will you keep me safe?" she asked with a smile.

"I shall do my best" James smiled back. He looked up through the glass blocks where he made out the shape of a taxi pulling up outside, "I believe your chariot awaits mi lady."

"Oh well, I guess I better be on my way before I turn in to a pumpkin."

"Off you go Cinderella. Hey, do you have money to pay for this taxi?"

"There are other methods of payment." She said.

Amelia turned away and walked towards the door just as Evelyn was coming in.

James opened his wallet and took out two £20 notes "Here" he said "Just in case the driver is old fashioned." He handed her the money.

"My knight in shining armour as always"

"Amelia!" James called after her; she stopped and looked back "Look after yourself."

"I always do" she said and swung through the glass doors.

Evelyn watched her go over her shoulder. She walked over to James with raised eyebrows, "What's going on?" she asked.

"What?" James shook his head and looked mystified.

"Well it looks like I've just seen you chatting to a known prostitute in the lobby of a police station then giving her money?"

"Just doing my good deed for the day, helping someone less fortunate than myself get home safe. Not jealous, are we?"

Evelyn laughed and almost spat.

"What did you find at the crime scene?" James asked.

"Not much, yet again. Whoever our killer is they must be a big CSI or Dexter fan because this scene was clean. However, we did find tyre tracks on the field where the victim was found. Vehicles are prohibited in that area so I've got uniform doing house to house. It would have been unusual for a car to be there and there are a number of houses that back on to that field. Someone must have seen something."

"Good. Can we get anything from the tracks?"

"Hmm, might give us a clue to the type of vehicle but it doesn't narrow it down much."

"I'll go and find Black. Fill him in, see if he has any ideas."

James turned to walk away, Evelyn dropped her hands to her side "This is our investigation!" she said "We don't have to consult him on everything."

James stopped and turned back "It was our investigation, and so far, we've been getting a new victim every day and its gone public. I'd say we need all the help we can get. Black used to be one of the best detectives on the force."

"*Used to be*, exactly."

"This guy has forgotten more about policing than you or I will ever know. We need him." James turned and walked down the corridor "Are you coming?"

"I need to type up my report from this morning."

"Suit yourself." James walked away leaving Evelyn standing in the lobby alone.

Chapter 39

Craig Underwood sat in his car. The heater was on but he was still shivering. He hadn't even bothered to go home tonight. He loaded up his car this morning then he had gone straight for a burger after work, although now he wished he hadn't. His stomach was churning. After the burger he'd just driven around, stopping, waiting for a bit, thinking, driving, stopping, waiting, thinking. He was now parked up in a lay-by. It was a quiet road, occasionally a lorry or car would squeeze past between the hedgerows but mostly it was just cows and green fields, and Craig, alone in his little car. Currently he was staring at his mobile phone, trying to compose a text message to his wife. She would be wondering where he was by now. He never did overtime until this late. He couldn't say he was playing squash again; it was fairly obvious he wasn't that keen a squash player he thought looking down at the straining buttons on his shirt.

The phone rang, it was his wife. For a minute he thought about not answering but he knew she wouldn't give up "Hello love…no I'm sorry the car's broken down….yeh I'm just waiting for the RAC….yeh I know, i…….i know I shoul…..i know I should have called but I've had no signal until now…..yeh I'll keep you updated…hopefully won't be too much longer. Yeh I'll let you know when I'm on my way…..see you soon." Craig switched the phone off and placed it in the glove compartment. Then he put the car in gear and drove back towards the town.

Tuesday 1st October 2019

Here's a recipe for you:

Take one frustrated bored middle-aged man

Stir in one frumpy nagging middle –aged wife

Add in a pinch of kinky sex curiosity

Crumble in access to the internet

Then fold in a good dollop of prostitutes who can fulfil fantasies to order

Mix vigorously

And what do we have? I guess you'll have to wait and see.

Chapter 40

It was cold. The first frost had fallen; the sky was clear and blue. The bin lorry growled and squeaked, the workmen stepped down from the back of the lorry, their high-vis jackets beacons in the grim alleyway. Two cats tumbled into a ball, squealing and whaling at each other. Takeaway wrappers scuttled down the street through urine stains and dried vomit. The binman pulled the bin away; he was used to seeing things that weren't pretty, the things that people threw in the bin, the things that missed the bin. This morning he saw something that made him shiver, made him break out in a cold sweat, made him throw his breakfast up on the pavement in front of him. There on the pavement behind the bins, kneeling naked, wrists handcuffed, throat slit, was the body of Craig Underwood.

*

The crowds were getting bigger, shouting louder. There was more press not just those from the local newspapers and regional TV news. The blog had become an internet sensation and the theory of there being two killers was now common knowledge. The story had national coverage; everyone was living in fear of the West Moors Killers. Reporters shouted and heckled James and Oscar as they ducked under the police tape and walked over to the white scene of crime tent.

James hadn't seen Evelyn since their argument yesterday; he had been in contact with her via email. She said she was following up a few leads so he left her to it.

As they approached the tent the officer in charge stepped aside to let them pass.

Craig was still in the position the bin man had found him in. He was on his knees with his back pressed against the wall. His head was tilted back so the wound in his neck was clearly visible. He had been posed that way on purpose, to shock whoever found him, to make sure he made it in to the papers.

"What do we have?" asked James.

"His name is Craig Underwood" said the officer in charge "he was a factory worker aged 43"

"How do we know?" asked Oscar.

"His wallet was wedged behind his knee cap." Said the officer "Looks like whoever killed him wanted to make sure he was identified."

James was agitated; the smells of the alleyway seemed amplified inside the small tent. He needed to get out.

He went back outside, Oscar followed him. There were a number of witnesses giving statements to the other officers when he saw a face he recognised. He walked over.

"So, you saw him?" James asked.

"Yeh I saw him" Amelia said "This is my patch, well the street around the corner, he comes around here often, you know you get to know the faces, the cars. He doesn't come to me though. I saw him drive down here really slowly, stop a couple of times talk to some of the girls. None of them got in the car with him though, then he got to the end of the street turned left, I think, or was it right? He drove away anyway, really fast like he had to be somewhere. Next thing I know a body had been found down by the bins. I was worried it was one of the girls so we rushed down before the police got here. When I saw his face, I knew I'd seen him before so I thought I better say something."

"Thank you" James said "You have been very helpful."

"A pleasure" Amelia said "As always."

James and Oscar walked back to the car. "Looks like he was a regular in these parts" said Oscar.

James buckled up his seat belt and started the engine "We need to talk to the wife see if she knows anything," he said as they drove away.

Chapter 41

Mrs Underwood sat in her armchair drinking her tea and shaking "I was angry with him." She said "He didn't come home last night. I called him about half six and he said his car had broken down he was waiting for the RAC. He said he was going to ring me when he was on his way home but he didn't ring. I tried to call him a few times but it just went straight to voicemail every time. I left him messages, I texted him, but nothing, no response. I thought he had another woman, I was furious, I've had my suspicions for a while, something wasn't right. He was out nearly every night and that just wasn't like him. He was a real home body or at least he used to be. He would just come home from work then plonk himself down in front of the telly and that was him for the duration of the evening, he barely moved. Even at the weekend he never really wanted to go anywhere or do anything, boring sod. Then these last few months he started going out nearly every night. Sometimes he'd say he was working overtime which was strange because he hated that job, then he'd say he was playing squash or going for a drink with people from work which was strange again because he was hardly a fitness fanatic and he wasn't exactly social. Still wouldn't do anything round the house though, lazy bugger. I've been nagging him for ages to sort the garage out but he kept putting it off, couldn't find time in his busy schedule to do something for me could he? I offered to do it myself but he kept insisting he'd do it." James and Oscar exchanged a look, "Mrs Underwood, how often do you go inside the garage?" Oscar asked.

"Well, never." Mrs Underwood said "It's just full of all his junk that's why I wanted him to sort it out."

"Mrs Underwood" said James "do you mind if we take a look inside your husband's garage?"

The metal door slid up and over with a screech "Oh my god" Mrs Underwood gasped unable to remove her eyes from the sight that confronted her, "Dirty bastard!" What she saw inside the garage was a range of paraphernalia including whips, ball gags, handcuffs, nipple clamps, ropes and a selection of knives.

"Mrs Underwood why don't you go back inside?" Oscar said "Our family liaison officers will look after you." Mrs Underwood was ushered back inside without speaking and without taking her eyes off the contents of the garage.

"I think it's fair to say Mr Underwood's new hobby wasn't squash" James said to Oscar.

"As his body was found in the red-light district I think I know what his recreational activities consisted of" said Oscar.

Something caught James' eye, something on a table sparkled. He picked it up. It was an earring, an earring with a blue stone.

"What is it?" Oscar asked.

"This earring looks just like the one belonging to Jenna Bishop, when we found her she only had one," James looked at Oscar "You said he was taking trophies."

James took a plastic evidence bag out of his pocket and placed the earring inside it.

"You think this guy could be one of the killers?" Oscar asked

James just stared back into the garage. "I don't know, maybe. What do you think?"

"Could be, especially if he has Jenna Bishops' other earring. Maybe the other killer decided the best way to win this sick game was to take out the opposition?"

James looked back at the garage and ran his hand through his hair "May be. I want everything in this place examined. If there is even a trace of any DNA from the other guy we need to find it."

Chapter 42

Oscar was back at his desk in his little glass office. He was trying to complete a report for an important budget meeting but he couldn't stop thinking about the murders or how it made him feel working on real cases again, going to crime scenes, examining evidence, trying to second guess the killer and knowing sooner or later you were going to outsmart him. Oscar felt alive for the first time in years. The alarm no longer felt like an instrument of torture. Now he couldn't wait to start the day. He would wake up early lying there going over the cases, trying to come up with theories, solutions, suspects. Drink no longer occupied his thoughts in the evenings, he enjoyed the feeling of a sharp mind, he liked waking up fresh and alert. Sometimes the darkness came back to him though. What if he failed? What if he had to face the responsibility that someone could lose their life because of his mistake? Just then there was a ping from his computer to let him know he had received an email. It was a reply to an email had sent. He saw the name, a name he knew well but he didn't open it.

He unfolded the napkin the waiter had given him, it had to mean something. Who was that guy, how did he know about the case?

There was a knock at the door, then it opened. Oscar knew it was James before he even turned around.

"People are turning up at crime scenes and taking pictures of themselves at the crime scenes then adding them in the comments section on the blog like this is some kind of sick game." James said.

"And then there's this" Oscar handed James a copy of the local paper. One the front page the headline read 'West Moors Killer Inflicts Terror On Small Town'. The article advised people to not only lock all their windows and doors but barricade them too, and sleep with some kind of weapon close to their bed regardless of what the law might say. The police couldn't catch this killer and they had to be able to defend themselves in case the killer did manage to get through the barricade and wake them in the middle of the night. It advised people not to go out at night unless absolutely necessary and take extra care when travelling to work or taking their children to school.

"Great" said James "That's all we need."

"Misery is money for the press, fear is even better."
"Well they've got fear in bucket loads," James said throwing the paper down on the desk "Where do we go from here?" he said looking out of the window.

"Actually, I have found something" Oscar handed James the folded napkin.

Chapter 43

"Are you sure is the place?" James asked.

"It's what it says on here" Oscar replied looking down at the napkin in his hand.

"What did he say we can expect to find here?"

"He didn't. He just shoved this napkin in my hand with this address on it and then he was gone. We have to check it out."

James looked up and down the street, "I've seen this before" he said "This was the last fare of Levi Archer. This is where he came the day he was killed. We investigated it but it was empty. No-one was registered as living here."

"Let's take another look then."

They stepped out of the car and into the rain; it had not stopped pouring down all night and as the sun began to rise the rain remained. The pavements were dark and slippery, puddles had formed in the uneven parts and they darkened further as the rain continued to fall. A jogger ran past and splashed in one of the puddles.

The house was at the end of a row of red brick terraces opposite the park. At one time this house had probably been a desirable address but the windows were boarded up and the paint peeled from the window frames. The front door had been painted green at some point, but that paint had almost completely disappeared and a few peeling shards was all that remained. The stained-glass panels in the door were either faded or broken. The rest of the houses on the street were now much the same. The brass numbers were still intact the number five of the 15 now swung upside down. Oscar pushed the door and it swung open without any effort.

"Well whoever has been here isn't all that bothered about security" James said.

They went inside; there was a narrow hallway with ornate cornicing on the ceiling that was now covered with black mould. Stairs lead up to the first floor and at the end of the hallway was a door that led to the cellar. To the right of the stairs a door led in to what must have at one time been the main living room with a large bay window and a period fireplace that were both now slowly degrading. There was no furniture in there just peeling wallpaper and broken floor boards. They moved quietly to the next room, another sitting room falling apart, there was a small kitchen off it with rain water pouring through the roof. It didn't look like anybody had lived here for a long time. Oscar and James headed up the stairs "Do you think we should call for backup?" James asked.

"I wouldn't recommend it, we don't have a warrant so we shouldn't really be here" Oscar replied.

They moved upstairs. What functioned as a bathroom was in a disgusting state. Oscar stuck his head around the door and looked around, it was empty. They moved on quickly to one of the bedrooms and pushed open the door. There was a mattress on the floor and a sleeping bag. Empty tins, bottles and newspapers were strewn across the room. "Someone's been here recently" Oscar said. He picked up one of the empty tins "There's food residue but no mould, someone must have been here in the last couple of days."

There was a noise. The noise of a door opening, it was the cellar door, someone else was inside the house. They heard the footsteps in the hall, the door closing behind them. There was a load bang, a gunshot fired into the ceiling. Silence. Then another gun shot.

James looked to Oscar hoping he would have a plan on what to do next. Oscar nodded towards the fitted wardrobe in the corner. They moved quietly and slowing, opened the wardrobe door and crouched inside.

"I knew we should have called for backup," James whispered.

"Too late for that now," Oscar whispered back.

The footsteps moved up and down the hall, then on the first stair, then the second, then they stopped. Then they started again but sounded like they were going back down.

The footstep moved down the hall faster this time and to the back. The door opened and closed again. Then just silence.

They waited a few minutes. It was quiet. Whoever it was had gone. They emerged slowly from the wardrobe, Oscar groaned as he straightened his back.

James was agitated "You think that was one of them? One of the killers?"

"I don't know" said Oscar "but whoever it was, they were unhappy about something."

"None of the victims had gunshot wounds?"

"Unless that's the next escalation?"

"Or a method of coercion?"

It was so quiet all that could be heard was the rain pattering against the outside and the occasional whoosh of the traffic rushing through the puddles on the main road beyond. They moved on to the next bedroom, it was dirty there was mould on the walls. The only light was the small slits from the boarding on the windows. They could both see it though. Hanging from a rope on the light fittings was the lifeless body of a young man. The rope twisted slightly and the light from the window revealed the man's face "That's him" Oscar said, "That's the waiter!"

Chapter 44

Tom Hodden liked to travel. He travelled to Kenya for his gap year before university then each summer he travelled to a number of places including Africa, South America and South East Asia. After he graduated he travelled to Australia, New Zealand, Singapore and Japan, all for different charities. Sometimes he was paid, sometimes he volunteered and he would get work in bars, cafes or fruit picking farms to pay his way. He loved it but when he turned 28 he decided maybe it was time to settle for a little while, stay in one place. He got a job working for a UK homeless charity; he started at nine in the morning and finished at five in the afternoon, Monday to Friday. At weekends he volunteered at a homeless shelter in the centre of town. As much as he liked to help people and he liked the stability of a steady income, the grey grim skies of home were starting to get him down. He went running every morning before work. His feet pounded the pavement. His feet itched, they itched for his old life, the sun, the sea, the people, new customs, new experiences, no routine. Every time his feet hit the floor they carried him further and further away.

Chapter 45

"There was a chair on one side of him like he'd kicked it away, which would suggest this was suicide, however it looks like he received a blow to the head." Oscar said. Forensics was scouring the dilapidated terrace house. They were both still stood in the bedroom were the body had been found. The body itself had now been removed but the mangled light fitting still remained above their heads.

One of the other officers walked in to the bedroom, "We found this" he said holding up a wallet sealed in a plastic evidence bag. "Looks his name was Wayne Smith, he was 19. There were some letters as well but they were addressed to a house in Birmingham and all about six months old. They're all either from theatrical agents or responses to applications from reality TV shows, all rejections."

James took the letters and looked at them. "Looks like he had a hunger for fame."

"That's what we've ascertained so far but we will do some more digging back at the station, see if we can trace his family and if he has any previous."

"Thanks" said James and the officer walked away.

"I think whoever killed the waiter was the same person who killed Vanessa Marsden. This has been done exactly the same. It seems he's running out of ideas" said Oscar.

"But who is he?" James asked "Why does he know about this? Another strange thing, he's not been added to the blog, no warning, no gloating, no pictures. Not so far anyway."

"I think he was working for someone else, that's why he's not been added to the blog. He wasn't part of the game, he wasn't meant to be one of the victims. He was punished because he broke the rules."

"He must have wanted it to stop that's why he approached you and gave you this address."

"I'm not so sure he did. Maybe he enjoyed the fame, the buzz of it. He wanted to make sure we didn't miss anything."

James looked out of the window; yellow police tape was being wrapped around the gates to the park across the road.

Thursday 3rd October 2019

Anything you can do. Well now the secrets out there isn't much point in pretending. I love how helpful people are in this town. Especially a big strong man like that.

Chapter 46

"This one's just been dumped, not staged. We don't know who he is yet, no ID on him but he's dressed in running gear and this is a popular running area." Evelyn had already taken control of the scene when James and Oscar ducked under the police tape and walked across the park towards her.

"You sure this one is linked?" asked James.

"His picture has just been added to the blog but we haven't got a name yet." Evelyn answered.

James looked around the park and back up at the house. He turned to Oscar, "What do you think."

"I think whoever it was that was hiding in the cellar of that house had something to do with this."

"What?" Evelyn asked.

"We were on our way to the station when we got the call about this. We have just been at another call across the road." He nodded over to the house which was now also wrapped in police tape. "We think we have another but it's been made to look like suicide."

"Was there a note at the scene or an update on the blog?"

"No but the victim approached Oscar in a Café and gave him this address."

"He told me our killers are competing" said Oscar, "That they are not working together but against each other, trying to outdo each other."

"And while we were checking out upstairs, someone emerged from the cellar and fired two-gun shots in to the ceiling. They must have heard us entering the house and tried to scare us so they had time to get away."

"Did you see them?" asked Evelyn.

"No" said James "but someone must have. I want to conduct a house to house see if any of the neighbours have seen anyone coming and going to that house, see if we can get a description may be even come up with an e-fit."

Evelyn looked down at the body in front of her, "Well looking at this I think that makes sense." She looked back at the house "that the address Levi Archer was called to before he disappeared wasn't it?"

James nodded, "which makes me more convinced that it must be linked." James crouched down by the body, "So this is definitely the latest victim?"

"Yes. He's been hit on the head with a heavy object, but there's no show, no staging, that makes me think the killer was disturbed." She walked around the body and scanned the park "Fitness fanatics train at all times of the day. Maybe this place wasn't as secluded as the killer hoped and they just dumped the body and left before anyone saw them."

"Or maybe they were planning on taking him to the house across the road and dragging him down to the cellar and doing god knows what to him" said Oscar.

"But you two got in the way" said Evelyn.

"Exactly."

James crouched down by the body and looked at it more closely "This guy looks in pretty good shape whoever he is; he wouldn't have been easy to carry." He stood up and looked back to the house where the waiter's body had been found "Maybe he was too heavy to be staged and that's why he's just been dumped here in this way. Maybe the killer has just lost their assistant."

Oscar stepped forward wagging his finger as if a light bulb had just gone off in his head "It could give us a clue as to our killer's build. They might not have much physical strength that's why they need help." Oscar thought for a second "The other victims who were mutilated were already unconscious, or already dead, when it was done."

"I think you're right" said James. "The guy hanging from the light fittings back there was the assistant to someone of a slight build. We need to find out who he is, and keep an eye on that blog. I want to know if any more updates appear."

Chapter 47

James threw the papers across the floor then stood up and kicked the chair he'd been sitting on. He was aware of Oscar and Evelyn turning to look at him. He ran his hand through his hair "Damn it!" he yelled. "Forensics have checked everything in Craig Underwood's garage and the rest of the house, there is no DNA from any of the victims except the DNA that was found on the earring of Jenna Bishop, that was hers. But there are no other trophies and nothing to lead us to any other suspects."

Evelyn got up and began picking the papers up off the floor, she placed them back on James' desk without saying anything. "Thank you" he muttered.

She smiled "No problem" she said.

James felt ashamed of himself. He was just so frustrated he didn't know where to turn; they had no leads, nothing to go on. The killings were becoming daily occurrences. How long before they escalated again? How long before there were two or three people being murdered every day? Everyone was watching him, waiting for him to catch these killers but he just didn't know what to do.

"Ok" said Oscar standing up "Let's think about this, we have two killers," he walked over to the white board and drew too columns and wrote killer 1 at the top of one column and Killer 2 at the top of the other. "Now we have been thinking they've been working together as a kind of tag team and that's why the murder's differed so much, but this competition theory actually makes more sense. They are working individually but competing against each other."

"How are they competing though?" asked James "I mean how are points awarded? Who decides who wins? And who is this guy Wayne the waiter? And what about Craig Underwood? He must have something to do with it? Why does he have one of the victims' earrings in his garage?"

"Hmm" said Oscar "That bit I'm unsure of. The murders did escalate. Isabelle Montgomery-Smith's was much more violent that Maureen Connolly's."

"But then Elizabeth Robertson was killed in much the same way as Maureen Connolly and Lucy Maxwell." said James.

Oscar looked back at the board. "Maybe it's not the method but the victim?" said Evelyn.
Oscar turned around "How do you mean?" he asked.

"Lucy Maxwell was a prostitute and drug user, the less dead, but the victims change each time, upstanding members of the community, charity workers."

"Like chess" said Oscar "it's not about the number of pieces you take but which pieces."

"Exactly" said Evelyn "they must score more points or something based on importance of the victim is or how good a person he or she is deemed to be."

"So how do we work out who could be next?" asked James.

Oscar looked back at the board, "Good question." He said.

He placed his hands on his hips and took a deep breath, "Anyone want coffee?" he asked. Oscar and Evelyn looked up astounded, James never made coffee.

"Not for me" Oscar said "I have to go soon."

"What?" said James "You're leaving?"

"I have a budget meeting" Oscar looked at his watch "Starting in two minutes." He began to pack his things up.

"What about the case? We need you."

"I told you I would help when I could but I have other commitments. I'm sure you'll be fine for a couple of hours, kids." He put on his jacket and left.

James opened his mouth to say something but thought better of it.

"I'll have coffee" Evelyn said holding up an empty mug.

"Ok" James picked up his mug then took Evelyn's and walked to the kitchen area at the back of the office. He put the kettle on, rinsed the cups then placed a teaspoon of instant coffee in each mug, then reached for the sugar when something occurred to him. He had worked with Evelyn for three months now and he had never once made coffee for her. Did she take sugar? Did she have milk?

He stuck his head around the door, "Erm…how do you take your coffee?"

She smiled, she had obviously been waiting for this question "White with one please."

"Oh right, yeh, of course" James said but they both knew this was the first he'd heard of this.

James handed Evelyn her coffee and perched on the edge of the desk opposite her. "Thank you" she said taking a tentative sip from the steaming mug.

"It's a pleasure" he replied taking a bigger drink and burning his tongue. He winced but tried to hide it in front of Evelyn.

"This is a tough nut to crack huh?" Evelyn said.

"You're not kidding. As soon as I think we're on to something they twist again and throw any theories or potential suspects we may have out of the window. All we've got is a faint hope that they'll make a mistake, leave some kind of forensic evidence or a clue to their identity. Maybe one of them will get arrogant and leave something that'll lead us to him on purpose so he can take the credit for this mission he's on, whatever that is."

"No slip ups so far though. Maybe our killers just aren't that stupid."

"Nah, they're not stupid. I'm hoping arrogance is the thing that will undo them. They are advertising what they're doing with this website. Sooner or later one of them at least must want to reveal who they are"

"Maybe you're right."

"I hope so because I really don't have anything else at the minute. We haven't got a hope in hell of finding these guys, let alone making any charges stick."

Evelyn placed her mug down on the desk and picked up a file "I think I might have something."

"Really? What?"

"Well it's just a theory, might be just a coincidence."

"There's no such thing as coincidence in police work, go on?"

"I've been doing some background checks on the victims. One thing they do all have in common is that they are all local. Then I checked their histories to see if any of them are linked in some way. I found out that all our victims have committed minor offenses in the last year, failure to pay council tax on time, driving offenses, parking tickets."

James stood up and looked at the paper Evelyn had in front of her and examined the details "Not really the type of thing that would make someone go on a campaign of justice." He said.

"No, well that's what I thought at first but then I came back to the local thing. During the past year all our victims have been featured in the local paper under the week in court section."

"Seriously?"

"Take a look." Evelyn handed him the newspaper cuttings. "Maybe it's not a motive for the killings as such but it might be how the victims are being chosen."

"And if we know how the victims are being chosen maybe we can work out who's next."

"Exactly."

"I want a list of the names of everyone who have appeared in that section of the newspaper over the past year, and their addresses. We will send squad cars round to keep watch and see if we can catch these bastards in the act before they kill again."

"That's a lot of names and a lot of resources. Won't you need to get that authorised?"

"Yeh, a formality." James picked up the phone and dialled an extension number "I need a meeting with the chief as soon as possible; I need an emergency operation authorising….ok I'll be up in five minutes." He hung up and straightened his tie and put his jacket on. "Right I'm going to beg our case to the chief. You keep working on that list."

"Will do Boss." Evelyn reopened her computer.

James ran out of the door and stuck his head back round "Good work detective." He said.

Chapter 48

The picnic area was fairly quiet; there was a couple who looked like they must be retired, trying to drink coffee poured from a thermos while chasing after a couple of toddlers, who Oscar assumed must be their grandchildren. He had been watching them while he waited for her. Despite their obvious frustrations they smiled and laughed a lot, those smiles seemed to wipe away the advancing years. Oscar thought about his own impending retirement, what would he have to smile about? What reasons would he have to leave the house? Would he come to places like this?

It was a cold day; the clouds lay heavy and grey in the sky and threatened rain but so far it was dry and so cold Oscar could see he was breathing heavily and quickly. He was nervous. It had been 20 years since he had seen her, she was just a kid then, she would be a grown woman now. How had she turned out? What would her life be like now? Did she still blame him?

He had wanted to meet in a café or somewhere they could eat and drink and discuss how good or bad the food was, discuss the café décor and how slow the service was, any subject other than that they had really met up to discuss. He knew it had to be done.

He didn't even think she would reply to his email, she probably didn't still access that account after all this time. He remembered the day he set it up for her. It was a rare in those days for a kid to have their own email address. He set up one for himself as well. "This is in case you ever need, someone to talk to, a grown up, for whatever reason you need. You just send me a message on here and I'll reply." She never did though, and he had been relieved about that. He had run out of things to say to her, run out of assurances to give. He didn't think she would reply this time, he hoped she wouldn't. He sat there in his little office and tried to convince himself that sending the email was enough, that he had tried, so good for him. She did reply though, she said she would meet him. James had asked him to help with investigation but he knew he had to see her before he lost his nerve so he lied and said he had a budget meeting. He knew neither James or Evelyn had any interest in budgets so they wouldn't check. Today he would have to see it through. He would have to face her.

"Thank you." Oscar said. He stood up and shook her hand; she gave a polite smile and sat down on the bench opposite him. She looked normal enough, she was slim but not gaunt like the last time he had seen her. She had not developed an eating disorder or become a drug addict as he had feared. Her blonde hair still looked the same, straight and long. She wore a navy trench coat and protected herself from the cold with a brightly coloured scarf wrapped around her neck. The large floral bag she carried suggested it might be used as baby changing bag. Her fresh skin made her look younger than she was but of course Oscar knew her real age.

He suddenly couldn't think of anything to say. After all the years of planning this conversation he was lost, there were no words that seemed adequate. She threw him a lifeline "how have you been?" she asked.

How had he been? He should be asking her that surely, "Good" he replied nodding "Yeh I've been good." He couldn't meet her eyes and instead looked at the ground. "What, what about you?" he asked nervously.

"Yeh I'm good" she said with a smile. She clasped her hands in front of her on the table and Oscar noticed a wedding ring.

"You got married" he said pointing at the ring.

"Yes, five years ago now. He's a nurse, we've got two children Lucy is three and Isacc is eighteen months."

"Must be a handful"

"Yes, but they're worth it, I suppose," she said smiling and rolling her eyes "Did you have any children? I always wondered."

"No" he said "No children."

Carrie took a deep breath and nodded; a child fell over and started to cry.

"It was just a small wedding" Carrie said "You know."

Oscar nodded. He knew.

"How's your wife?" Carrie asked.

"She died, cancer, five years ago now."

"Oh, I'm sorry to hear that." Carrie reached over and patted his arm.

"So, it's just me, I'm thinking of getting a cat though so then I can say it's me and the cat."

Carrie smiled, "Yeh I've said that one a few times."

"Really?"

"Yeh I was alone for a while before I met Robert. It was hard, you know. They sent me to a therapist, my foster parents. Between them and the social workers they didn't think I was forming relationships properly. My school teachers agreed, can't say I blame them though."

"Why?"

"I did get in to trouble quite a lot I suppose. I didn't mean to, I just had all the anger inside me. If someone looked at me wrong or tried to use my pencil I'd just go nuts. Like I needed to let the anger out. That's what the therapist said anyway."

"Yeh that sounds like therapist speak. I've been sent to one of those before."

"Why?"

"When my wife died, work thought it might help me deal with the grief. I only went twice then I skived it."

"You should have given it a go. I was sceptical at first but it did help."

"Where did you meet Robert?"

"At university. I was a mature student, I'd kind of messed up school but like I said the therapy really did sort me out, eventually. I decided I was sick of lurching from one dead end job to another and I wanted to get my degree. Robert was the only other mature student on my course so we kind of bonded."

Oscar smiled "I'm glad. I really mean it, you deserve to be happy. What do you do now?"

"Well we both studied nursing but I'm just taking a little break at the moment. What about you? You still with the police?"

"Yes, Detective Superintendent now."

"Well done."

"Well it's mostly pen pushing, well it was, I've just got on aboard with a new case, one last final fling."

"Final fling? How come?"

"I'm retiring soon, well, early next year but may be sooner."

"But if you're involved in a live investigation why would it be sooner?"

"The Chief wants me out. Truth be told I don't blame her, I've become something of a liability over the years."

"You've worked hard for a long time, you should see it as a blessing. Life is short, I know that, you should seize every opportunity and don't be ruled by work."

"Maybe you're right. Are you sure you don't want a drink or anything?" Oscar said "there's a van over by the play area that sells tea, coffee, sandwiches, ice cream."

"I'm fine really. I've got to pick the kids up from nursery soon, so…"

"Right" Oscar nodded and looked back down at the ground. He knew he had to get on with it. He had asked her here after all, she wanted to know why.

"I'm sorry" he said.

"What are you sorry for?"

"I made you a promise. I promised I'd find the person who killed your family, and I didn't."

"You did your best."

Oscar gave a small nod. Did he do his best? This was the question that had kept him awake at night for the last twenty years, the question he had searched for an answer for in the bottom of a whiskey bottle.

"I used to be angry. Angry at them, angry at you, angry at my family for not defending themselves better, angry at myself for not being there, just angry at the whole world. But I realised that being angry wasn't going to bring any of them back. It wouldn't change what happened.

Happiness is the best form of revenge, I have my own family now. I've moved on, I've let go. You should too."

"He's still out there though."

Now it was Carrie's turn to look at the floor. "I can't think about that. There are a lot of evil people out there that don't deserve to be walking free."

Oscar nodded silently, he knew she was right.

"I really do have to go" she said glancing at her watch. She stood up and stepped over the bench.

"Thank you, again" Oscar said "I really mean it. Talking to you like this today has really meant a lot to me."

"Oscar, don't let them win. They don't deserve to win." She smiled and turned away, walking back toward the car park. Oscar watched her walk to a shiny red car, this year's registration. She must be doing ok he thought. Then something occurred to him.

"Wait!" Oscar called after her as he scrambled up from the bench and jogged across the car park to where she was standing "What do you mean *they*? You said *they* don't deserve to win?"

"Well…. I just mean whoever they are; I don't think anyone who can kill a whole family really deserves anything good to happen to them." She laughed nervously.

Oscar stared at her for a moment. "Do you know who did this Carrie?"

"I really have to go." She turned on her heel and started walking, faster this time. Oscar ran after her.

"Wait!" He caught up with her and grabbed her arm, "Do you know who did this? Do you know who murdered your family? Does it have anything to do with the killings that are happening now?"

She couldn't look at him "Some things are better left in the past." She yanked her arm away and got in to her car.

"Carrie!" Oscar called after her but she started the engine and drove away without looking at him.

Oscar got in to his car and drove home. He had hoped he would be able to sleep better that night, that he would somehow be absolved. Now his mind was racing more than ever. If Carrie knew who the killer was, if she'd known all along and not told anyone, maybe it meant that he could stop blaming himself. But why would she do that? Maybe she was afraid the killer would come after her but it had been twenty years, surely if that had been their intention they would have done it by now? Twenty years. These other murders had started the day after the anniversary appeal in the newspaper. Carrie had said they, plural, could these be the same killers?

He had to find Carrie again, find out what she knew.

Chapter 49

James sat down and adjusted his tie, "I need some extra resources authorising, it's urgent."

The Chief placed her pen down on the table and looked at him. "It must be a lot of extra resource if you've come to see me?"

"It is" James said "My colleague has established a link between the victims of these serial killers and people who have appeared in the 'This Week in Court' section of the local paper. She is drawing up a list of other potential victims at the moment and I'd like to place each one of them under surveillance for their own protection and also because we may be able to catch the killer in the act."

The Chief rested her chin on her hand without reacting "Have you done a costing for this?" she asked.

"No, I mean not yet. I haven't had time. My colleague only just established the link and we need to dispatch the patrol cars now."

The Chief went quiet. She picked up her pen and ran it through her fingers "This would take you way over budget and this investigation is still ongoing. I'm sorry DCI Miller I can't authorise this."

"This case is huge; it's on the national news and on the front of every paper every single day surely you want us to be seen to be doing everything we can?"

"Of course. Once this case is solved it will put our little force on the map, however it means that everything we do is being scrutinised, not just this case. We still have to remain within budget constraints."

"But the next victim could be one of the people on that list!"

"You can't be sure of that. To offer police protection to every single person in the borough who has appeared in court over the last year would be an outrageous cost and would cause panic. You'll just have to think of another approach." She pulled out another piece of paper and started reading it.

James could feel his face burning. "Thank you for your time" he said through gritted teeth and left.

*

James walked back in to his office and kicked the waste paper bin across the floor.

"Not good news?" Evelyn peered over her computer screen.

James gripped the back of his chair and stared in to the middle distance "She said no." he said flatly.

"I've been working on the list; it's getting pretty big already maybe she's got a point."

"This is the first lead we've had. What does she want from us? She's on my back for not having any leads then when I get one she won't give me the resources I need to pursue it."

"It might just be a coincidence, or maybe I could be wrong?"

"No" James sighed exasperated "You did a good job. I still want the rest of those names; we'll have to keep an eye on them as best we can." James looked out of the window down in to the car park. A few people were getting in to their cars and going home. "Do you fancy getting out of here?" he said "Let's call it team building."

"Sure" Evelyn said. "I'll get my coat."

Chapter 50

Oscar stood by his car. The smell was different. It was autumn now, and there was freshness in the air. It's funny, he thought, how autumn can be seen by many as more of a new start than January. It smells of more possibility. That day it was early summer and the air was hot and thick. He remembered the drive down, still in the same car he drove today, no air conditioning, the windows rolled fully down. He had taken his jacket off and loosened his tie but his shirt still clung to him with sweat.

He looked up at the house, it still looked the same. Maybe there were a few more loose tiles and maybe the paint had peeled a little more, maybe the window frames had rotted a little further but apart from that it still looked the same, untouched. As far as he was aware it was empty. The housing company that had developed the land around it didn't even want it. They said they had already had trouble selling some of their properties because the land was so close to what happened. It put people off, knowing what had happened there, some people even believed the site was haunted. The house had been put on the market but the only people who came to view it were tabloid tourists and journalists who wanted to be in the place where it happened. He wondered what Carrie did for money if she had been relying on the sale of the house. He wondered if she had ever come back here like he had today to face the demons.

He left his car where he had parked it at the end of the lane and walked down the path to the front door. It wasn't even locked. When he turned the handle it just opened. He supposed even burglars didn't want to come in here. The hallway looked the same. He remembered on that day there had been a ticking clock, today there was silence. He assumed nobody had been back to wind the clock or the battery had died and there had been nobody around to replace it. Carrie had been sat on the stairs, wearing her school uniform, hugging her knees. She smiled when she saw him "Do you want a cup of tea?" she said, "Oh I'm not sure if I'm allowed to use the kitchen yet."

"It's ok, it's too warm for tea anyway" he told her. He remembered her eyes darting back to the kitchen. He asked her again what had happened, what she had seen. She told him calmly and matter-of-factly. "Is there anyone who might want to hurt your family Carrie?" he'd asked, "Someone with a grudge?" She shook her head and stared towards the front door.

An officer at the top of the stairs signalled to him, "Carrie why don't we move in to the living room, it's a bit comfier in there." he said. They stood up and he steered her towards the living room and sat her down in a chair with her back to the hallway. He talked to her about her day, about school. She answered simply and politely, behind her he saw them carrying out the body bags. The two adult ones went first then the three small ones behind them.

Oscar walked in to the kitchen. It was dark. The bushes outside were overgrown and kept the kitchen in shade. The chairs were still there neatly tucked under the table. She came in here, he thought, she saw the sandwiches half eaten the drinks half drunk. He shivered.
He walked around the room so neat and quiet but thick with dust. Who are you? He thought, who are you who could do such a terrible thing then just disappear. He knew why no-one want to live there they thought whoever had done this was still hanging around somewhere.

When he finally ushered Carrie into the police car he placed his hands on her shoulders and looked in to her eyes "I'll get whoever did this." He said. She just looked at her shoes.

He had lied though; they had gotten away with it. Even if he caught them now they had had their life it had been twenty years.

Oscar walked out of the kitchen and hovered at the bottom of the stairs. He didn't want to go up there but he needed to see that room again. He walked up the stairs slowly, each step creaking, his heart racing. He got to the top and opened the door to the main bedroom. The curtains were closed; he walked around the bed and opened them. This is what Carrie did, he thought. He turned his back to the window and looked at the room. It was bare, clean. The only furniture that remained was the bed frame; the mattress had been taken away, the carpet too. He had seen that room so many times in his nightmares, heard the way the blood squished in the carpet. There were only floor boards now but he could still make out the odd stain. He took a deep breath. He had done it. He had come back.

Chapter 51

James took the quickest route out of the town centre to avoid the lollipop stops and school run traffic. He took a winding road up in to the moors away from everything. The clocks would be going back soon but for now the sun was still high in the sky and it was bright and sunny and warm. He pushed a button on the dashboard and the roof of the car retracted. Evelyn shrieked with delight and grabbed her scarf which almost blew away with the sudden rush of wind.

James loved these roads. They reminded him of the roads in a car advert, curving bends and not another vehicle in sight. They travelled further up into the hills, nothing but grass and moorland around them. They rounded another bend then they were looking down in to the lush green valley below. There were a few houses clinging to the hillside in rows and at the bottom the reservoir glinted in the sunlight.

"Wow" Evelyn whispered.

"Sorry what was that?" James yelled above the rush of the wind.

"This view is amazing" she yelled back, "You would think we were in the middle of nowhere, not just a few miles from work."

"You would indeed." James spotted a lay-by at the side of the road and pulled over. "Follow me," he said. He got out of the car and crossed the road, Evelyn followed as he lead her down a steep path that meandered through the long grass. At the bottom there was a small flat plain of grass that looked like it could have been a terrace cut in to the hillside, ahead there was nothing but rolling hills and blue sky.

"You can see the sea from here on a clear day like today" said James "Look."

Evelyn walked up to the edge and stood beside him and looked out at the grey-blue smudge in the distance "Oh yeh" she said, holding up her hand to shield her eyes from the sun.

"I love this spot" James said "I used to come up here with my mum." He sat down on the edge of the terrace and let his feet dangle over the side. Evelyn sat down next to him. "We used to live down there" he said pointing down in to the valley. "We would walk up here all the way through there" he pointed to a meandering path "And when we made it all the way up here we'd stop and have a picnic."

"Local boy then?"

"Ha, Hoddlesworth born and bred me. That's why I jumped at the chance to transfer here from GMP when I got the offer. This is my home; it's in my interest to serve it well."

"Was it just you and your mum?" Evelyn asked.

"Yeh my dad never came."

"So, your dad wasn't around?"

"Oh, yeh he was around, still is, but he was never interested in spending time with us, well not with me anyway." James leaned back on his elbows and took in the view.

"My Dad was a bit like that" Evelyn said "He was just always working."

"Mine was the same."

"It was just me and my mum most of the time. For all the use she was."

"You don't get on?"

"No. she died, a few years ago now."

"I'm sorry."

"It's ok, like I said we weren't exactly close. She preferred spending time with her friends above spending time with me. She was part of every community volunteer group that existed and she packed me off on every hobby she could think of. When she was at home she spent her time baking or making her own Christmas decorations, the perfect housewife."

"I suppose she just wanted to keep everything nice for you."

"I guess. I think her motivation was more about impressing the neighbours than keeping us happy" Evelyn played with the crucifix around her neck nervously. "Well I'm free of her now." She looked away from James and back out at the valley.

"Parents eh?" James said.

"Yours must be proud of you Detective Chief Inspector."

"You'd think that" James said with a laugh. "I don't think my dad's ever been proud of anything I've done. He won't be proud until I have a wife and kids and a soul-destroying job, then come home and sit in an arm chair and moan about how soul destroying my job is. Just like him."

"What does he do?" Evelyn asked.

"He's retired now but he was an accountant."

"Mine was a lawyer, wanted me to follow in his footsteps. I tried for a while, did the first year of a law degree but then decided to do Criminology instead."

"What did your dad say about that?"

"He said it was my choice, I think he was a little disappointed though. Mum made it very clear that she thought I was wasting my time. I think she was just worried about telling her friends at the WI that her daughter was a drop out." She laughed a little.

A large bird of prey flew above them and circled. James thought it might be a hawk. They both lay back and watched it. It circled above them a few times, then it stopped and hovered for a minute or so. Neither of them spoke they just sat and watched the hawk; suddenly it swopped down from the sky and pounced on something in the long grass further down the valley. A few seconds later they saw it rise up and fly away in to the distance.

"I guess we better be heading back." Evelyn said "or else the chief will be on your back for wasting resources again."

"And we don't want that."

They got up brushed the grass from their clothes and began walking back to the car. As they set off the sun was low in the sky and turned it a hazy orange colour.

"Is it on the cards then?" Evelyn asked.

"Is what on the cards?"

"The wife and kids?"

James laughed, "Not any time soon."

"Has it ever been?"

"It was once, nearly."

"What happened?"

"You ask a lot of questions." James turned down a bend in the road.

"That's my job. To ask questions, interrogate people."

"And you are very good at it indeed." James paused and kept his eyes on the road, he realised she wasn't going to give up. "She was on the force too, we met in training. She was good, better than me. One day when she was just starting out in uniform she was called to a murder scene. A woman's body had been found in some woods, she had been stabbed. It was Rachel's job to secure the perimeter. A witness had seen the attack, the guy who did it had run away, CID checked his address but he wasn't there. He had camped out in the woods all night. He still had the knife and when he saw Rachel on her own he ran out and stabbed her, only once, but it was enough. She was dead before the ambulance arrived." James swallowed hard, his eyes fixed on the road. "After Rachel died I made up my mind I was going to quit. I was AWOL for two weeks, just going out drinking, staying home drinking, waking up alone and hung-over then going out and doing it all again. My mother pleaded with me desperately to get help; grief counselling, tell the doctor how I was feeling, get a sick note, take a proper break. My father just rolled his eyes and walked out. Well he had just found me slumped on the floor covered in vomit wearing the same clothes I'd been wearing for the past three days, so maybe he was justified on that occasion. It was Rachel who had sorted me out eventually. At her funeral her parents gave a eulogy talking about her love of the force, her desire to see good triumph over evil, like she was a superhero. I looked at her photograph by the side of the coffin in her police uniform; she looked like a superhero, to me anyway. I had been letting her down; she would want me sober, out there catching as many bad guys as I could. After that I sorted myself out. My boss at the time had been sympathetic and decided not to put me through any disciplinary procedures. I've worked hard consistently since then, always trying to prove myself, go above and beyond and always getting results, until now."

"I'm sorry" Evelyn said.

"It's the risk we all take."

"I guess so."

They turned another bend and the town came in to view at the bottom of the hill. It glowed as the street lights were beginning to be switched on.

They drove the rest of the way in silence. Not awkward though, suddenly they were two people who knew each other well enough to not have to say anything. It was a good team building exercise James thought, yes that's what it was.

Chapter 52

Oscar hit the brass door knocker down hard. He had checked the police file; this was her last known address he had to try it he had to speak to Carrie find out what she knew. He waited a moment, then he knocked again. A fragile old lady possibly in her 80s answered, she looked flustered by his insistence, "Can I help?" the lady asked.

"I'm looking for Carrie" Oscar said then realised he didn't know her married surname "she lived here with her husband and two children."

"I'm sorry" the woman said "I don't know who you mean. I just moved in here with my daughter. She's lived here for the past five years."

"Do you know where I can get in touch with the previous residents?"

"No, no I don't I'm sorry."

"No problem." Oscar turned and walked down the path.
He got back in to his car and banged the steering wheel hard with his fists. She was running scared that meant he was right, she did know something. At the time there were suspicions that it could have been Carrie that murdered her family. When they arrived at the crime scene she was numb, quiet. There was no crying or wailing or screaming, she just sat very still on the stairs and answered their questions. She obligingly offered to make tea for the crime scene officers. Psychologist's reports concluded that she had been in shock and the screaming and crying would come later, but it didn't. Not as far as far as Oscar was aware, but then, he hadn't made much effort to keep in touch with her over the years. Besides Carrie had an alibi, she had been in school at the time of the killings and a fifteen-year-old girl couldn't have murdered five people, her own family, could she?

Oscar drove away, who else could there have been? He was back to this question again. There was no extended family, both parents were only children and both sets of grandparents were dead. Carrie was put in to care after the murders where she stayed until she was eighteen, he assumed. But she was 35 now and had only got married five years ago. What had happened to her in those interim years? Why would she protect the killer? Surely, she would want to see them brought to justice, unless she was scared they would come after her?

He'd looked in to her eyes that afternoon when the bodies were found, placed a reassuring had on her shoulder "I'll get whoever did this, I promise." He told her. She just stared back at him blankly. Maybe she knew then that he was lying, that this killer would never be caught.

He turned the corner at the traffic lights and headed back to the station. One thing he was certain of was that there was a connection between the murders of that family and the murders that were happening now. As they had been unable to get a conviction or even identify any suspects, the killings had been attributed to an intruder. But nothing had been taken, there were no signs of forced entry and the house had been left perfectly tidy. There had been no signs of struggle. It seemed the family had just lay down and allowed their throats to be slit. He had always thought there was more to it but the thought had driven him almost to the brink of madness and he had chosen to console himself with a bottle of whiskey. He was sober now though, more than sober, he was eager again. The security gates to the police station car park opened. He was going to figure this out, if it was the last thing he did.

Chapter 53

It was late when James finished working. He was still at a dead end but he decided enough was enough; there was a Champion's League game on tonight, if he left now he might just be home in time for the highlights. He could flop on the sofa with a nice cold beer. Evelyn had left hours earlier; she had been quiet since they got back. Maybe he had said too much, given too much away. He knew this case had already caused him to drop his cocky façade, he was clueless and he was tired of trying to cover that up.

Oscar had never returned from his meeting, maybe it had run over, or maybe his heart wasn't really in the job any more like people said. He had been a great detective once though, and that drive, those skills, must still be in there somewhere. James turned shut down his computer and grabbed his jacket and his car keys. He walked through the station, it was quiet. A lot of the rooms were in darkness. There were a few people on the night shift hanging around but the station seemed bare. He walked through the front doors and across the car park. It was quiet out here too, hardly any sounds of traffic, people are staying indoors, he thought.

James was restless. Too restless to sit and watch TV and drink beer like everything was normal. He turned at the lights and followed the road back up on to the moors. He had forgotten until that afternoon with Evelyn how much he enjoyed being up there and how long it had been since he spent any time there. He had decided to sell the house after Rachel died, some people had told him he should keep it that it was full of memories, but James didn't see it like that. To him they weren't memories they were promises, broken promises of memories yet to be made. It was

Rachel who had fallen in love with the house; she had seen it as more than a house but a home, what would be their family home. James hadn't been that bothered either way but he wanted Rachel to be happy. After she had gone all he saw were empty rooms and bare walls. He moved on to a string of bachelor pads and a bachelor lifestyle but never really settled anywhere.

Work was his rock now. he kind of felt that it always would be somehow that nothing else could compare to it, and it was so demanding he couldn't imagine any woman other than Rachel ever really understanding what he did.

He was driving higher and higher, up in to the hills. He knew these roads had high death rates. There were flowers and tributes tied to fence posts all along these routes. It was the thrill that excited him, especially in the dark. There were no streetlights up here. All he could see in front of him were the bends in the roads where they caught in the headlights.

Something caught his eye in the rear-view mirror. It was set of headlights, it wasn't often you saw another car up here especially after dark. The headlights came closer; he accelerated a little to put some distance between them but the car behind accelerated too. It was close now, right up against the bumper; he could hear the revs getting louder and louder. His car jolted forward as the car behind rammed in to it. James gestured and shouted in to the rear-view mirror but the car jolted him again. James pushed the accelerator pedal to the floor, the car moved forward up the steep hill but the car behind him went faster too.

James could feel the sweat dripping down his brow, he had completed the intense driving course, in a town or a city there would be side streets he could take a detour, do a U-turn but out here there was nowhere to go except forward. The headlights illuminated the top of the hill, there was a bend but it was sharp and the car was going too fast. He pulled the steering wheel down hard to the right, the car screeched and everything went dark.

Chapter 54

James sat up, he could feel something wet in his eye, he knew it had to be blood. His car was a few feet in front of him upside down, the headlights still staring in to the darkness. He had managed to jump free of the car as it went over the edge and in a split second something made him close the door hoping that whoever was chasing him would assume he was still inside. The other car was still on the road above him; he could hear the engine ticking but could tell the car was stopped. Someone got out, he heard footsteps on the gravel, they stopped, and he waited, leaning back in to the wild moor grass as far as he could. His breathing suddenly seemed very loud to him, he tried to control it but it just got louder and faster. All he could think to do was hold his breath and stay as still as he could. The footsteps moved closer, James could tell by the sound that they had moved from the road on to the grass, he held his breath tighter. The footsteps stopped. There was nothing but the sound of the ticking engine in the darkness. Then the footsteps moved again first thudding on the mud and grass then crunching on the stones and concrete. The car door closed, the engine revved and the headlights moved, the sound of the engine drifted further and further away. James let go of his breath and gasped as if he had been held under water. He could still hear the hum of the car's engine but it was getting fainter now.

*

He could feel the blisters on his feet when he finally reached a residential street that was well lit. It was quiet now, just the odd car rumbling past. He had left his mobile in his car; he decided not to go back for it, that it was safer to just keep moving as quickly as he could without drawing any attention to himself in case whoever had been following him was still watching. He stayed away from the road and crossed the moorland heading in the direction of the town. Now he was in the light he could see his trousers were soaked and covered in mud, amongst other things. His coat was covered in pieces of grass and heather. He spotted a phone box at the end of the street. He couldn't remember the last time he had used a phone box but James did have a special skill which he was very proud of, he always memorised every number in his mobile. He felt around in his pockets and thankfully found some change. He first thought to call Evelyn but then he remembered her daughter, it was late, he thought better of it. Instead he called the only other person he could think of to help him. It rang twice then a voice answered "Oscar?" James said "I need your help. Again."

*

The tea was luke warm and too weak but it tasted like the best tea James had ever tried. "Thank you" he said to Oscar as he handed him the polystyrene cup.

"So, can you tell me again why you called me at this hour and why when I arrive to pick you up you're dressed as a hobo?" Oscar asked.

"I was followed. A car followed me up on to the moors and ran me off the road; I had to walk back across the moors to town. Ouch!" the nurse pulled the thread of the stitch towards her.

"Almost done" she said with a cheery smile.

"You think it was them or one of them?" Oscar said.

"I don't know, it could have been, I didn't get a good look at them though, it was dark."

"All done" the nurse said placing her instruments back on the trolley, "I just need you to sign a few forms then you can go." She pushed the trolley away and left the cubicle.

"My face has been all over the news" James continued "it's no secret that I'm in charge of this investigation. It been quiet for a few days, no updates no murders, may be these two are not so keen on getting caught after all." James hopped down off the bed and headed for the reception desk.

"It's not like anything I've ever seen before" said Oscar. "Serial killers have worked in pairs before but usually they collaborate with each other, not compete with each other."

"I wonder if there are any rules to this game and whether running me off the road counts as one."

They walked back through the waiting room. It was the early hours of the morning but the waiting room was still busy. In the corner was a large man, obviously drunk, with a bandage stuck to a cut on his head. He kept slipping in and out of sleep but he sat up when he saw James and Oscar.

"Oi!" the man called "Oi! What you doing here? You should be out, working, trying catch this killer! You should be doing your job properly! Oi!" The man attempted to stand but ended up falling back in to his chair and mumbling.

"Ignore him" said Oscar. "I'll take you home. Look on the bright side, at least you don't have to drive that hideous BMW anymore." He slapped James on the shoulder as they walked out of the hospital doors.

"At least my car wasn't rescued by the Ark!" James said as they headed across the car park.

"You can wait at that bus stop if you want?" Oscar said pointing across the road "I think the number nine should be here in about five hours."

"It's alright I'll slum it in this antique, just this once." James smiled as he opened the car door.

They drove back in silence with James drifting in and out of sleep. Occasionally he would open his eyes and think he saw someone, standing in the street, hanging around, watching. Is it you? He thought to himself.

Oscar pulled up outside James' apartment building. It was quiet, most people were still in bed, a van drove by, James jerked around to look at it but it just carried on driving.

"Try and get some sleep," said Oscar "We'll recover your car in the morning with any luck if his car hit you there might be some evidence."

"Yeh maybe." James opened the door and got out of the car "'I'll see you in" he looked at his watch "well a few hours." James closed the door and waved as Oscar drove away then walked wearily inside. He lay on his bed still in the muddy damp clothes he'd been wearing all night. He thought about taking a shower, about curling up under the crisp clean white sheets but instead he just fell in to a deep dreamless sleep.

The alarm buzzed at 6am. James groaned as he turned over, normally he was up at 6am to do a workout but not today. Today his legs ached from his night time trek across the moors and the stitch above his eye throbbed. He put the alarm on snooze and rolled over. His phone beeped. This time it was a message. He tried to ignore it but curiosity got the better of him, he picked up the phone. The message was from Evelyn, she wouldn't be able to come in today, her daughter wasn't well. 'No worries' he replied.

He decided he might as well get up; he wasn't going to get back to sleep now anyway. He showered then stood and stared at himself in the mirror. It was quiet outside, still early. He dressed, on the outside he looked the same as ever apart from the gash above his eyebrow but something had changed. It wasn't just the general public at risk any more, he was at risk too. He looked in to the mirror "Who are you?" he said out loud.

Wednesday 9th October 2019

Silly silly boys. I loved the story in the newspaper. You think your so clever, this next one will clinch it. I will be the winner.

Chapter 55

Melissa Anderson had it all, beautiful house, wonderful husband, great job, and a perfect child. Since having Millie she had gone part-time at work as she wanted to be a perfect mother, but didn't want to lose the independence or the sense of achievement she got from her job. She had worked in PR since leaving university, where she met Daniel. They met in the SU bar during Fresher's Week and they dated all the way through university. They both got good jobs pretty much as soon as they graduated, Melissa working in PR, Daniel working for an accounting firm. They bought a flat together a year later, then a year after that Daniel proposed. They married 18 months later and had the perfect wedding, horse drawn carriage, church service, reception in a grand country house hotel and a honeymoon in Bali. It wasn't long after that Melissa found out she was expecting Millie. It was then that they decided to move to a bigger house, this house. It was brand new, four bedrooms, detached, with a large driveway double garage and a big garden for Millie to play in.

Now Millie was at school it meant Melissa had more time to herself on the days she didn't work. She would go to the gym, make sure her perfect beautiful house was spotless, get her nails done, catch up with her friends who also only worked part-time and then pick Millie up from school, which is exactly what she did today. She came running out to her across the playground her uniform still a little too big for her, waving a picture she'd drawn for her. "Wow that's beautiful sweetheart" she said as Millie handed her the picture. She took Millie's hand and they walked home while Millie told her mother about her day. There were times when Melissa found this boring but then she reminded herself how lucky she was and she smiled. She had the best of both worlds because her husband had a good job and could afford to support her while she worked part-time. Even after ten years together she still got butterflies when she saw Daniel at the end of the day. She still found him attractive and he adored her. She never had any reason not to trust him, he would never be unfaithful, she knew a lot of women said that and were proven wrong, a lot of her friends has said that about their husbands and been proven wrong and they laughed at Melissa when she said it with such surety, but Melissa knew she was different, her husband was different, her life was perfect.

When they got home, Millie wanted to go and play in the garden, she loved the new swing set Daniel got her for her birthday. Melissa gave Millie a drink of milk which she downed in seconds she was so eager to go and play. She let her go while she prepared dinner for that evening. She looked up through the window over the sink as she washed the carrots, Millie was swinging happily. Melissa peeled the carrots and placed them to one side. She looked back to the window and smiled, she took some peppers out of the fridge then went back to the sink to wash them, she looked back to the window, the swing still went back and forth but Millie was gone.

Chapter 56

James walked in to the incident room and began circling it while looking at the board hoping somehow, he would coax out some information that might lead him to this killer. Oscar walked over to the window and looked out. It was getting late, it had been a long day, no more murders but they knew there was going to be one soon, they had to try and figure out who it could be. They had continued with Evelyn's work going through the list of people who had appeared under the 'This Week in Court' section. Then had gone back a year as that was the earliest any of the victims so far had appeared, the list ran in to the hundreds though and they had no way of figuring out who the next victim could be. It could be any of them.

James stopped in the middle of the room, put his hands over his head and sighed. Oscar put his hands in his pockets and leaned against the wall. Neither of them said anything for a few minutes.

"Let's go for a drink." Oscar said finally.

"Seriously?" said James "with everything that's going on?"

"Especially with everything that's going on. We need to unwind, where's Evelyn?"

"She didn't come in today; her kid was ill and couldn't go in to school so she had to stay at home and look after her."

"Right well you go around there and see if the kid's made any kind of recovery and I'll meet you both in the Kings Arms in half an hour. First rounds on me." Oscar put his coat on and headed for the door.

James followed quickly behind him, "I won't argue" he said.

Chapter 57

Carrie walked back down the road from the car hire centre. She had been careful to park her own car far enough away so no-one would see it. She climbed in the battered old ford fiesta and drove away. It was dark now. She drove further and further in to the night until there was no main road just winding country lanes, no people, and no other cars. She spotted a phone box and pulled over. She slipped the cheap ring she had been wearing on her wedding ring finger off and placed it in the glove compartment, it had done its job. It had been convincing. She walked to the phone box and dialled the number she knew so well. A voice answered "It's me" Carrie said "It's done. Yes. I think so. He seemed happy, content, thinking that I was alright. No,.no. he didn't ask anything like that." Carrie played with the phone cord nervously "So is that it? Can I go now?I don't know, just away from here, I don't ever want to come back here…..Thank you." Carrie sighed and put the phone down. She got back in to her car and drove away. She didn't know where she was going; she just drove on and on until the darkness swallowed her.

Chapter 58

James knocked on Evelyn's door; he could see her stood in the hallway talking on the phone. She hung up then came to answer the door.

"Hey" he said with a smile.

"Hi" she answered pushing her hair behind her ears "What are you doing here?"

"I brought some sweets for the patient" James said holding up a pink stripy bag.

"Oh right. That's very kind of you." She paused and looked around. "Erm, come in then." She moved aside and James followed her in to the hallway. "The patient isn't here though I'm afraid."

"Oh really."

"Yeh, she was feeling better so I sent her to her dad's" Evelyn put her hands in her pockets and rocked back on her heels. "Do you want coffee?" she asked.

"Yeh sure that'd be great." James followed her in to the kitchen. Evelyn's house was perfect, neat methodical, like her desk at work, nothing was out of place. There were no ornaments no knickknacks no pictures on the walls.

Evelyn filled the kettle with water and switched it on. Then she took the cups out the cupboards and measured the coffee out, she didn't need to ask him how he had his coffee she had made it many times.

"We missed you today" he said. He had missed her, but he didn't want to say that out loud.

"Really" she asked over her shoulder as she poured milk into the cups.

"Yeh, I think me and Oscar are going to kill each other if we're left alone too much."

Evelyn laughed. "It was your decision to bring him in," she turned to James, "I liked it when it was just me and you." The kettle boiled. Evelyn turned and poured the hot water in to the cups.

"We weren't getting very far though." James saw Evelyn prickle, he felt bad, he knew she was proud of her work "I mean it was a complex case, a unique case, helps to have a bit more experience on board."

Evelyn handed James his coffee "Do you really think he's up to it though?" she said "I've heard people say he had a bit of a drinking problem."

"He used to, after his wife died I think. He's sober now." Evelyn took a sip of her coffee "This is a stressful case. He could relapse."

"It was grief. Greif does strange things to people." James drank his coffee and didn't look at Evelyn. There was a silence. "So, can we expect you it tomorrow?" he asked.

"Yep. Ready and raring to go, Boss."

"Where's your car anyway?" he asked "I didn't see it on the drive?"

"Oh, it's in the garage. Bloody thing. Nothing but a money pit."

"Do you need a lift in the morning?" James asked

"No, it's ok I'll get the bus."

"Are you sure? It's no trouble?"

"No. No thank you but really I'm ok on the bus."

"Anyway, the real reason I came around..."

"You have a 'real' reason?" Evelyn said with a smile.

"Oscar wants you to come out for a drink, well he wants the three of us to go, said it'll be good for morale."

"Oh"

"Come on, I think he might be right, and your patient isn't here for you look after anymore."

"I'll get my jacket."

"I'll drive."

"You'll have to."

Chapter 59

The pub was small and dark, what some might refer to as an old man's pub. It was on the end of a row of terraced houses, the bar area looked as if it could have been someone's front room. It had probably once been a second home to miners and factory workers who lived in the houses along the row and simply poured their wages back in to the pockets of their employers.

It was decorated in wood panelling with brass fittings. Behind the bar there was a mirror with various logos printed on it in green and red. There was a juke box on one wall and a fruit machine opposite; a couple of men were playing darts against the far wall. James and Evelyn swung through the doors and spotted Oscar sat at a table in the corner, he waved to them and they walked over. He was sitting in the corner of a booth under a window with three drinks on the table in front of him, a pint of larger, a glass of red wine and a glass of orange juice. James and Evelyn shuffled on to the seats opposite him. "Cheers Oscar" said James picking up his pint and taking a large gulp.

"Thank you, Oscar," Evelyn said as she took a tentative sip of wine.

"I thought this would do us some good" Oscar said "This case is pretty heavy and no-one is pretending it's not serious but we need to stay level headed about this like we would any other case. We can't be seen to be getting dragged down and start to panic like everyone else."

"But this case is unique" said Evelyn, "when has there ever been another case involving competing serial killers?"

"Not one that I know of, but we can't keep thinking about it like that, like it is so unique there isn't a way of solving it. It's a murder investigation; we've all worked on murder investigations before."

They looked at each other, then back down at their drinks. "We can do this" said Oscar. James and Evelyn smiled.

The night played on. James and Oscar did battle over the juke box, it was a duel between Oscar's selection of Northern Soul classics and James' pick of Oasis and The Stone Roses.

"This is rubbish!" Oscar bemoaned as the final chorus of Live Forever rang through the pub for the third time that evening.

James held both hands up and looked to the ceiling as if he was experiencing some sort of divine intervention. "Soon be your turn again" James said "Then you can bore us to death with your old man music."

"And that is just what I am going to do" said Oscar as he stood up fishing the change out of his pocket and walked over to the juke box.

"Fancy another?" James asked picking up Evelyn's glass.

"Not for me" she said reaching for her jacket "I have to get going."

"Oh, right, well, I better get my keys."

"You'll do no such thing, officer; you've had far too much to drink already."

"But I drove you here" James said.

"It's fine there's a cab office just across the road, I'll get a taxi."

"But..."

"There are two serial killers on the loose? I'm aware of that and I dare one of them to try and tackle me." She zipped up her jacket and smiled.

"Ok, well, be careful and text me when you get home." James said.

Evelyn gave a mock salute "Will do sir," she said "See you tomorrow Oscar"

"Yes, see you tomorrow Evelyn" Oscar replied.

"Bye" she said to James and left.

James turned to Oscar and picked up his glass, "Same again?"

"Ah maybe I'll be a devil and get a blackcurrant and soda this time" said Oscar.

"Coming right up." James took the glasses and walked over to the bar. He returned with the two drinks and flopped down on the bench next to Oscar "I don't know what we're doing, I don't think we'll ever get these guys." He said.

"Try keeping your voice down" said Oscar, "People are panicking enough."

"I don't blame them," he said and picked up his drink took a big gulp then placed it back down on the table. He looked down at the glass "Do you miss it?" he asked Oscar.

"Working on a live investigation?"

"No. Drink?"

Oscar picked up his blackcurrant and soda and swirled the ice around so it clinked on the side of the glass "Every second of everyday," he said.

"It takes a lot of guts to keep fighting like that. Resisting temptation in a place like this."

"You just have to keep reminding yourself why you quit in the first place" said Oscar.

"And why was that?"

Oscar laughed and down his blackcurrant and soda in one, "Sometimes I wonder," he said.

*

It was late, last orders had long since been called and James was leaning on Oscar's shoulder as they left the pub "Come on let's get home" said Oscar.

"Nah" said James, "Let's get a kebab."

Chapter 60

James wasn't sure what time it was but as soon as he opened his eyes his head was thumping. He closed his eyes again and wished it away but he knew it was futile. He sat up slowly holding his head, he felt his stomach flip and he swallowed hard. He turned to sit up, he put his feet on the floor and felt something cold and slimy squelch between his toes, he cringed and his stomach flipped again. He lifted up his foot and examined the damage, the remains of cold and congealed donner kebab clung to his bare skin. He looked around for some tissues, spotted some on the coffee table and wiped his foot. He didn't recognise the room. Through the thick velvet curtains the sun peeked in, the wallpaper was floral; there was a chocolate brown leather sofa and a battered teal armchair that didn't seem to match. There were a lot of knickknacks and ornaments around the place and a chess board set up on the coffee table in front of him. Some of the chess pieces had been moved as if there was a game in progress.

He could hear someone in the kitchen then the living room door opened and Oscar walked in dressed, clean shaven, carrying a tray containing two cups of coffee and a glass of fizzing Alka Selza.

"Morning" Oscar said cheerfully.

"Morning" James mumbled.

"I thought you might need this" Oscar said handing James the Alka Selza.

"I do indeed, very much so" James swirled the glass then downed the contents in one. Oscar picked up his coffee then sat back in the armchair and smiled.

"One of the few pleasures of being a reformed alcoholic is taking joy in the hangovers of others, it's not often I get the chance to feel smug.

James picked up the kebab tray from the floor, placed the tissue inside it, closed the lid and placed the tray on the coffee table. "Well far be it from me to deny you this pleasure." He picked up his coffee and drank it tentatively.

"We needed last night though," Oscar said.

"Easy for you to say," said James. "You stayed sober." He rubbed his head and motioned to the chess board "Who's your opponent?"

"Ivan, from Kentucky. We play online, he's winning, again. I'm not very skilled but it's a good distraction, stops me thinking about other things. He's got me in a zugzwang situation."

"What's that?"

"It means it doesn't matter what move I make the consequence will be a loss, but it's my move so I'll have to act soon."

Oscar looked at the board for a minute; there was a knock at the door. Oscar got up to answer it and left James hunched on the sofa sipping at his coffee. He opened the door and saw Evelyn stood there and angry expression on her face.

"I've been trying to get hold of you for the last hour, and James" Evelyn said "Neither of you were picking up. I've been round to James' place but he's not there, do you know where he could be?"

Just then James appeared at the side of Oscar still in the clothes he'd been wearing the night before "Right here" James said.

"Oh, for goodness sake, look at the state of you. Why didn't you answer when I called?"

"Sorry my battery must be dead." James said.

"Mine too" said Oscar "what's happened?"

"We've had a missing person report, The Chief asked us to check it out in case it's linked to our investigation" Evelyn paused "It's a kid this time."

James rubbed his head again "Give me five minutes" he said and went back inside.

"Come in" Oscar said to Evelyn moving aside from the door.

"It's ok I'll wait in the car" she said. She seemed agitated, kids did that to some people especially when they were parents themselves, "Make sure he gets a move on" she said as she turned and walked back down the path. Oscar gave a mock salute as Evelyn had done the night before and went back inside.

Chapter 61

"Can you just tell us again in your own time, exactly what happened?" Evelyn said sympathetically as she placed a cup of well sugared tea into the shaking hands of Melissa Anderson.

"I was in the kitchen preparing dinner. We had just walked home from school and Millie wanted to go in the garden and play on her swing. I gave her some milk and I let her go. I was in here the whole time and I could see her from the window." She pointed to the window over the sink. "She couldn't have been out there for more than five minutes and then I checked back again and she was gone. The swing was still going so she couldn't have been gone long. It was still going, back and forth, back and forth, back..."

"Then what did you do?" Evelyn interrupted.

"Well at first, I just thought she was playing somewhere else in the garden so I went outside and called her name but I couldn't see her anywhere, then I noticed the side gate was open so I went into the street and called, and called but...." her voice started to break.

"Would Millie often open the gate and go and play in the street?" James asked.

"No, she knows he's to stay in the garden unless one of us is with her. Besides she can't open the gate, the latch is too high she can't reach it."

"And the gate was definitely closed?" said Evelyn

"Yes, I always make sure the gate is closed, always!"

"Then what happened?" Evelyn continued.

"Well I checked out at the front, checked the garden again, checked the house, checked with the neighbours but no-one had seen her. That's when I called the police."

"And when did you call your husband?"

"After I called the police, I haven't been able to get hold of him though, he often travels around for meetings, he can't always answer his phone if he's driving. I've left him loads of messages though so he should be home soon."

James motioned to Oscar to join him in the kitchen, "This doesn't fit" James said "This kid couldn't have been in court over the last year, her parents weren't on the list either."

"It was only a theory" said Oscar "It's unusual for a five-year-old to be missing over night; something is going on here we need to stick with it."

Daniel Anderson clattered though the front door, his designer suit was crumpled his face was red and sweaty. "What's happening? Why are the police here?"

"Where have you been?! I must have left you a dozen messages! Millie's gone missing!"

Daniel's face fell "What? When?"

"Yesterday afternoon. She was playing in the garden then I looked up and he was just gone."

"Where were you?"

"I was in the kitchen! I only took my eyes of her for a second and she was gone. Where were you? I was ringing and ringing."

"I had a meeting, I must have left my phone behind, I'm sorry, I'm sorry I'm not blaming you I'm just trying to work out what happened. Come here."

He embraced his wife and she sobbed in to his shoulder "it'll be alright" he said "sshh now. She's probably just gone off exploring or something you know how inquisitive she is. She'll be back when she's hungry." Melissa nodded but looked unconvinced.

"Mr Anderson do you mind if we ask you a few questions?" Evelyn asked.

"No not at all" said Daniel.

"Do you know of anywhere your daughter could have wandered off to? Any particular places she liked to go exploring?"

"No not off the top of my head. My wife might know?"

"We've already asked your wife these questions we just wanted to know if you had anything further you could tell us. Mr Anderson please can you tell us where you have been all night?"

"I've been in work, I had a meeting in our Redditch office, it finished late so I stayed and decided to drive back early this morning while the traffic was quiet."

"Anyone else attend that meeting?" asked Evelyn.

"erm, no I never actually made it. There was traffic on the motorway"

"I thought you said the meeting finished late?" James said.

"It did, I caught the last few minutes then one of my colleagues de-briefed me."

"So, you just sat in traffic on the motorway for most of yesterday?" said James.

"Am I on trial here? Look I stopped at a service station for a sandwich I have the receipt here somewhere to prove it" he felt around in his pockets looking for the receipt he checked the inside jacket pocket and found it. "Here it is" he said with joy but at that same time his mobile phone fell out of his pocket and on to the carpet.

James bent down and picked up the phone, then looked at it for a moment "I thought you said you left your phone at the office?" he said.

Daniel just looked at his phone and said nothing, his face started to twitch.

Chapter 62

The dog barked "Hush Fred". It barked again and walked on, he called after it. It was a cold morning a frost had fallen and the leaves that remained on the trees looked clean and crisp. He liked to walk his dog at this time of day. The sun was just rising and the orange light danced on the sparkling leaves. It was quiet apart for the odd growl of a passing car on the road above; the morning rush hour had not yet got in to full swing. All that could be heard was the rushing of the river, the breaking of crisp twigs beneath his feet and the tuneful singing of the birds. He walked deeper in to the woods, the dog ran ahead, a magpie squawked. He walked further, deeper in to the wood, it was darker here the leaves on the trees stiffened and blocked out much of the sun.

"Fred!" he called. He waited. He expected to hear the rustling of bushes, paws on fallen leaves, panting and cheerful yapping. Nothing. He called again. Still nothing. He moved forward through the dense woods, he had lost the path completely. He was aware of the sound of his own breath, the sweat on the back of his neck despite the cold. He broke through the last of the trees and found himself on the path by the riverbank. The sun was higher in the sky now and brighter. It danced on the flowing water beyond. He heard Fred bark and he sighed. He looked around and laughed to himself, he felt silly for being so afraid. Fred was further down the path barking and wagging his tail. "Come on boy" he said. He turned and started walking down the path towards the bridge. Fred continued to bark and stayed where it was. "Come on" he said glancing at his watch; he would be late for work at this rate. The dog barked louder and more forcefully "Fred!" he said getting frustrated. Still the dog continued to bark, he sighed and walked back down the path towards the dog, the frost was starting to melt now his feet squelched in the mud "what is it?" He stopped. There in the mud he could make out a shape and some clothes, some tiny clothes.

Chapter 63

Melissa came in with a tea tray complete with biscuit selection, "Here we go" she said and set the tray down on the coffee table.

"You didn't need to do that darling" Daniel said.

"It's fine" said Melissa "I wanted to."

"Sir" one of the other officers called James over and whispered something. He raised his eyes to the heavens.

Melissa began pouring the tea, "Who takes sugar?" she asked whilst trying to smile "Anyone for a biscuit?"

"Mrs Anderson, I think you should sit down" James said.

"Just one second" Melissa as she began passing around cups of tea.

"Mrs Anderson" James said "I really think you should sit down"

Melissa stopped and looked down at the cup of tea in her hand "But, I need to give everyone their tea" she said.

"Please" James said motioning to the empty seat on the sofa next to her husband.

Melissa sat down, her husband tried to grab her hand but she pulled it away.

James took a deep breath "Mrs Anderson, Mr Anderson I regret to have to tell you that a body has been found, the body of a child. We have yet to make a formal identification but we believe it is the body of your daughter."

Melissa Anderson howled in a way James had never heard before. She crumbled, her arms wrapping around her head, her legs folding until she was a ball on the floor. Her husband consoled her, remaining strong, stone-faced.

"It's my fault, it's my fault!" Melissa wailed, "I should never have let her out of my sight."

"Now stop that" said Daniel "Stop it! She was only in the back garden, you had no idea this was going to happen, you had every reason to think she should have been safe there."

Melissa snivelled and fiddled with the sleeve on her jumper, she shook her head and looked at the carpet, "If only, if only I'd …" her voice trailed off in to sobs.

Her husband made her stand up straight and put his arm around her "There's nothing that can be done now" he said matter-of-factly.

Chapter 64

Evelyn walked in to the incident room; James and Oscar were stood by the board talking. "What do you think then?" Evelyn said.

"Well he lied to us about where he was at the time of the murder" James said "So he must be hiding something."

"Which interview room is he in?" Evelyn asked.

"Number four" said James "Oscar I want you in with me on this."

Evelyn felt her jaw tighten "Erm, I thought I was your partner on this investigation?" she said.

"You are but if this guy is one of our killers I want Oscar's experience. It's nothing personal but we have to do this by the book, we can't let this guy slip through our fingers on a technicality."

"Look, I'm not trying to step on anyone's toes here" said Oscar.

"You're not!" said James and Evelyn in unison.

"It's not a question of that" James said while staring at Evelyn, "It's a question, of getting a result, potentially getting a serial killer off the streets." James looked away and sighed, then looked back at Evelyn, his eyes softer this time, "I hope you understand."

Evelyn smiled, "Of course" she said.

Oscar and James left the room. Evelyn watched them go. She sat back down at her desk, her fists clenched.

Chapter 65

The room was small, there were no windows. Daniel sat down, James and Oscar sat opposite him. James clicked the tape recorder and dictated who was in the room. "Is this really necessary?" Daniel asked.

"We just need to ask you a few questions about the murder of your son, can you tell us where you were between 12-3pm yesterday?"

"I already told you I was stuck in traffic on the M6. I have a receipt from the service station."

Oscar took out the receipt and looked at it "The receipt said you were at Knutsford services at 12:40" he said, "That would still give you plenty of time to get home before 3:20 when your son went missing."

"I stayed there for a little while, strolled around, stretched my legs. I'd been sat in a traffic jam for three hours."

"Anyone that can verify that?" asked James.

"I was on my own"

"Did you speak to anyone in the service station that might remember you?" said Oscar.

"No"

"Did you contact your office and let them know you missed your meeting?" James asked.

"No, I was going to but…"

"Because we spoke to your office" James interrupted "And they said you don't work there anymore? So maybe you should try explaining why you felt the need to lie about where you were today?"

Daniel was starting to sweat; he loosened his tie and took a big gulp of water.

"No comment" He said.

James just stared at him and Daniel took another gulp of water.

"Where were you today Mr Anderson?" James said his eyes still fixed on Daniel.

"No comment" Daniel said again this time louder.

"Listen" said Oscar "We know you are going through a tough time and you have our deepest sympathies for your loss. All we want is to find out what happened to your son. In order to do that we need to know every detail about everything that happened today."

Daniel looked at them both for a really long time "My wife can't find out," he said.

"Your domestic affairs are your own business Mr Anderson" James said "All we want to know is what happened to your son."

"I was fired three weeks ago; my wife doesn't know. I've been trying to find another job, that's where I was yesterday. I went for an interview. But I knew that wouldn't take all day so I told my wife I had a meeting and drove down the motorway to up the mileage so she wouldn't suspect. I stopped at a couple of service stations so I'd have some receipts,"

"Is there any particular reason why your wife would want to check up on you so closely?" said Oscar.

"No, she never has really, it was just in case."

Both officers paused. "Are you being unfaithful to your wife Mr Anderson?" said James.

"What? No! Why would you say that?"

"You obviously have a guilty conscience about something? You seem to be very well practiced at covering your tracks." Said James.

Daniel looked down at the table and shook his head "No. Nothing like that. I just didn't want her to know I'd lost my job. She has become accustomed to a certain lifestyle. She would hate me if she knew"

"Knew what?" James asked.

"That I was fired"

"Of course. Why were you fired Mr Anderson?"

"There were a number of factors"

"Such as?"

"Time keeping, poor performance."

"So, you had a warning? This didn't come as a shock to you?"

"No"

"But you still didn't think to tell your wife?"

"I thought I could sort it out, look I'm not here to talk about my work history I want to find out who murdered my daughter."

Oscar spoke softly "We know there's something you're not telling us Daniel. Something you want to get off your chest."

"I've told you everything I know; can I go now? My wife needs me."

"You are free to leave any time you wish Mr Anderson." Said Oscar

Daniel hesitated then quickly stood up and began to walk towards the door.

"How long have you been paying prostitutes for sex Mr Anderson?" said James.

"What?" asked Daniel.

"Your car number plate showed up on the number plate recognition system in the red-light district. In fact, it showed up several times." James passed a piece of paper across the table.

Daniel sat back down "does my wife know?"

"We haven't said anything to her as yet"

"It was only meant to be a one off. I met her in a bar; I didn't know she was a prostitute, at first. I'd gone out for a drink after work she was sat at the bar on her own. There was just something about her, I can't explain it, and she just enchanted me. The others moved on to another pub but I made some excuse about having to go home and instead I went over to talk to her, I just knew I had to. She told me her name was Venus; I guessed it wasn't her real name. It became obvious what she was but I didn't care. I started seeing her regularly, it was like a drug, I needed her. It wasn't that I didn't love my wife, it's just Venus was so different, so free."

"So, was it because of her you started cruising the red-light district? Looking for a hit?" said James.

"No, it wasn't like that. I just wanted her. I hadn't been able to get hold of her for a few days so I went there hoping I'd see her."

"Is this obsession with this woman the reason you lost your job?" asked Oscar.

"I couldn't think of anything else, she was the only thing on my mind. Always. I've been so stupid and I deserved to be punished for it."

There was a knock at the door James stood up and was handed a piece of paper by a uniformed officer. He stared at it for a minute before mumbling to the officer that he could leave, then he sat back down at the table.

"Mr Anderson, could you explain how your finger prints came to be on a pair of handcuffs found on the body of a recent murder victim?" James asked.

Daniel went white and took another gulp of water.

"No, no comment."

James handed the piece of paper to Oscar "Mr Anderson this victim was a Mr Craig Underwood. He was also a frequent user of prostitutes and was well known in the red-light district. His body was discovered yesterday morning; can you tell us where you were?"

"I think I want to call my lawyer now" Daniel said.

"Did Craig use the same girl as you?" said James

"Don't talk about her like that"

"Your girl, the one you were so obsessed with that it cost you your job. I bet you hated the thought of her with other men, her telling them all the things she told you just because they paid her"

"Shut up!"

"Because that's all she was doing, you know that don't you? This was no love affair it was all in your head. All she did was provide a service she was paid for."

"No, it wasn't like that I didn't pay her!"

James sat back in his chair and looked at Daniel; he was puzzled "You said she was a prostitute?" James said.

"She was, still is I guess, but she never took any money from me. I was different."

Chapter 66

Six months earlier

Glasses clinked, there was a smash as one fell to the floor. I think it was mine but I didn't care. The room was packed it was a Friday, one of the first nice days of the summer. A lot of people must have decided to go for a drink after work. It had taken me fifteen minutes to get served at the bar; I squashed myself between people, edging my way to the front until my fingers touched the edge of the chrome. Then I gently eased my weight forward until I was facing the bar then I leaned over slightly trying to get the bar staffs' attention. The heat was oppressive. I wanted to take my jacket off but there was no room. The staff looked hot and flustered too. I didn't envy them. Eventually I managed to get the attention of one of them, student type, looked like he was constantly thinking of better things he could be doing, but he served me, not with a smile though and I had no intention of giving him a tip. Suddenly she was there. She sat alone at the end of the bar. She sat up perfectly straight and sipped her drink serenely as if the rest of the carnage and the heat was nowhere near her, like she was protected in her own little bubble. I think she had what some people call poise, like a 1950s film star, immune to the stresses and degradation of the real world.

"There's your change mate." I think the bar man said to me.

"Keep it." I replied. I didn't care about his attitude anymore; I couldn't take my eyes off her, not even for a second. Then she saw me, she saw me starting at her. I was mortified but I couldn't look away, it was as if she had hypnotised me. I was under her spell already. I didn't know what she would do, most girls offer a rude hand gesture in that situation, well, they do to me anyway. I got the impression she wouldn't do that, she seemed too refined, too regal. Instead she just raised her glass and smiled at me. I think that must have been when I dropped my glass. I put the rest of them on a tray and fought my way through the crowd to get to her, spilling most of the drinks on the way.

"Are you thirsty?" she asked when I approached her.

"What?...oh." I looked down at the tray of drinks and laughed "No, these aren't all for me, it was just my round."
"I see." She smiled and nodded across the bar to where my workmates were standing. "Won't they be waiting for you?"

"Let them wait" I said. She smiled wider; she had a beautiful smile, like nothing I'd ever seen before. She seemed like she was from another world.

"Do you work around here?" she asked.

"Yes, we just came in for a drink after work."

"I gathered" she said while eyeing my crumpled suit "Do live locally?" she asked.

"Fairbanks. Do you know it?"

She took a sip of her drink and nodded "I know of it." She said.

I guessed she meant that she knew it was a family area and I most likely had a family. I thought that might put her off but she didn't seem all that bothered about it.

"I'm Daniel." I said offering her my hand.

She took it and then thought for a second "Venus." She said.

"Well it has been a pleasure to meet you Venus, and what do you do for a living?"

She took another sip of her drink then gave me another smile "I'm in the service industry." She said.

Chapter 67

Oscar poured the coffee James stood next to him closely "So what do you think?" James asked.

"There's something more going on here, something he's not telling us." Oscar said as he stirred his coffee deep in thought. "He's hiding something. We need to keep pushing him. Did you notice the 'no comment' getting louder? He's agitated. Let's get back to it. We don't want him to calm down too much. Keep doing what you're doing, when you ask him a question keep eyeballing him then say nothing else. Chances are it'll make him uncomfortable and he'll want to fill the silence."

"You think he killed his own kid? You think this could be one of our killers?"

"Maybe. Maybe not" said Oscar "His fingerprints were on the handcuffs we found on Craig Underwood's body, an earring belonging to one of the victims was found in Craig Underwood's garage, he knows something. He's starting to crack, He's on edge and then the story of how he met this Venus, he wants to talk. Keep pushing."

"Ok" James downed his coffee and placed his cup back in the sink.

They went back in to the interview room. Daniel sat at the table his head in his hands. He looked up as they walked in "Can I go now?" he asked.

"We just have a few more questions we'd liked to ask you first" said Oscar.

Daniel looked back down at the table.

James unbuttoned his jacket and placed it on the back on the chair. He moved his seat a little further back from the table to stretch out his legs. He looked at the piece of paper in his hands. He took a sip of water. "Mr Anderson, did you know Craig Underwood?"

Daniel ran his hand through his hair. "No. No I didn't know him I've already told you this." He said.

"We appreciate that Daniel" said Oscar as he leaned across the table "but we have a pair of handcuffs on the victim's body with your finger prints on them and we need to establish how they got there."

Daniel put his head in his hands again, his breath was heavy, loud. It sounds like he was about to burst in to tears. "Alright" he said "Alright. You're right I knew Craig. Craig Underwood was one of Venus's client's, one of her regulars. He treated her like she was nothing, less than nothing just there to fulfil his sordid needs." He rubbed his hands together like he was trying to wash them and stared into a spot on the floor in the corner of the room "I knew there was a hotel where they used to meet. Venus told me Craig was married and the things he wanted to do required space, privacy. I wanted to meet with her that night, I had a terrible day, more job rejections and I needed to see her. She told me she couldn't because she was meeting Craig at the hotel."

Which hotel?" asked James.

"I don't know, some grubby hotel."

"You don't know? You said she always went there with him, you found your way there you must know the name of it."

"I can't remember"

"What happened when you got to the hotel?" Oscar said calmly.

Daniel became fixated with the spot on the floor again "She told me the room number, I knew it well. The girl on the reception desk was playing with her phone; she didn't even look up at me as walked past. I went to the room, I stood outside the door, I could...I could hear them. I banged on the door, it was him that answered it, she was on the bed. I saw what he was trying to make her do." Daniel went quiet then looked at the floor. His breathing was steady, controlled he still didn't say anything.

Oscar and James looked at each other. Then suddenly Daniel kicked the table over knocking them both off their chairs then he got up and ran out of the door.

James stood up quickly "Get him!" he called to the officers outside. Oscar struggled to his feet "Are you ok?" James asked.

"Yeh, I'm fine" Oscar said breathlessly, "Quick get after him"

They both ran out of the door; two uniformed officers had apprehended Daniel at the end of the corridor and were holding him on the floor "You said I could leave anytime I wanted" Daniel yelled.

"Yeh well that was before you assaulted two police officers" said James.

The two uniformed officers picked Daniel up and held his hands behind his back with his face to the wall. Daniel looked down at the floor then banged his head against the wall.

"I did it" he whispered.

"What?" said James.

"I tied Craig to the bed in the hotel room, slit his throat, handcuffed his hands behind his back, drove him to the red-light district and dumped his body behind the bins. She begged me not to, she was worried I'd get into trouble but I couldn't stop myself." Daniel drew in a deep breath and choked back tears "And Millie. That's down to me too."

James caught his breath "Daniel Anderson, I'm arresting you for the murder of Craig Underwood and Millie Anderson. You do not have to say anything but it may harm your defence if you do not mention when questioned something you later rely on in court. Anything you do say will be used in evidence. You can wait in the cells until I've drawn up the charge sheet. You might want to get in touch with that lawyer, and your wife." The uniformed officers dragged him away.

Oscar and James walked back in to the office in silence. Evelyn jumped up from her desk, "What's happened?" she asked.

"We've made an arrest." Said James "Daniel Anderson confessed to murdering his daughter and Craig Underwood. I want to let him sweat it out in the cells overnight then tomorrow we can question him about the others."

"Well that's brilliant!" said Evelyn "The Chief will be pleased; did he say anything about who his accomplice or opponent is? Was it Craig?"

"We're not sure" James said "He did mention a prostitute called Venus he was with when he murdered Craig but he said she tried to stop him."

"Well that might make sense" said Evelyn "A lot of serial killers who kill in pairs are male female pairings; Fred and Rose West, Ian Brady and Myra Hindley."

"I thought we'd established that they weren't a pair that they were competing against each other?"

"We did, I'm just saying we shouldn't rule out the possibility that this Venus might be involved somehow."

Oscar had sat back down at his desk and remained silent since the arrest had been made, he was thinking, then he spoke "Why his daughter?"

"What?" asked James.

"He told us why he killed Craig he was jealous, straight forward crime of passion but why his son? Why the others?"

"Well like I said we'll question him about the other in the morning, I need to write this up."

James sat back down at his desk, one of the secretaries walked over to him "There was a phone call for you" she said "A lady by the name of Amelia? She said to let you know she is in hospital. "

Chapter 68

Oscar picked up the remote the coffee table. He could hear the hum of the microwave cooking his ready-meal in the kitchen. Daniel had confessed. Yet something still didn't feel quite right. Something still didn't add up. Why did he do it? Oscar knew better than to ask questions of why in a murder enquiry. That was the injustice most people felt, even more than finding out who did it, they wanted to know why they did it. It was also something Oscar knew couldn't always be answered, sometimes you just never found out why. This case was different though, here he felt that there really needed to be more of an explanation. Daniel Anderson had been a successful man, who was he competing with?

The microwave pinged. Oscar went in to the kitchen and poured molten cheese and tomato sauce on to a plate. He took another look at the packaging, apparently it was meant to be lasagne. He sat back down in his arm chair and shovelled food in to his mouth mindlessly. He starred through the window and watched the sun dip down behind the horizon, the sky darkened. This isn't over, he thought, not yet.

Chapter 69

James eyed the chocolate bars on the shelf; he didn't know which one she would like. She was so tiny he couldn't imagine her ever eating chocolate, he didn't think he'd ever seen her eating it, in fact he didn't think he'd ever seen her eating anything. Somebody bumped into him and the flowers he was holding crumpled a little. "Sorry" he said as woman in a dressing down shuffled past him. The hospital shop was small and he was in the way. He grabbed a bar of Dairy Milk from the shelf and took his place in the queue behind the woman in the dressing gown. The queue shifted slowly. Most of the people in the queue looked like they were patients in the hospital glad for a reason to stretch their legs and have a conversation; they were in no rush to get back to their beds. James eventually made it to the front of the queue, he handed the chocolate and the magazines he had selected to the woman behind the counter along with the money. He kept looking around him, he knew he shouldn't be here but he couldn't help himself, he had to see if she was ok.

He took the lift from the hospital lobby to the 3rd floor, ward seven. That was the information she left in the message, she must have wanted him to come or she wouldn't have called. The corridor was long and grey and smelt of bleach. There were windows one side that were currently being pelted by the seemingly constant rain. On the opposite side of the corridor were a number of doors. James passed them examining the signs until he reached ward seven. The nurses' station was on the right and to the left was a hand sanitising unit; he balanced the flowers, magazines, and chocolates under one arm and rubbed the anti-bacterial gel into his hands. James looked up and down the ward hoping to catch a glimpse of Amelia. He couldn't ask the nurses or check the charts as he had no idea what her surname was and he was fairly certain Amelia wasn't her real first name either.

He spotted her in the bed at the far end of the ward, the curtain was pulled partially open, she spotted him too and gave him a small wave, he nodded in recognition. He walked towards her and rounded the gap in the curtain, she smiled "For me?" she said gesturing towards the gifts James was carrying.

"Who else?" James answered and placed them on the cabinet next to her bed.

"Aw you shouldn't have."

He still wasn't sure why she'd called him. He looked again at the bedside cabinet devoid of any gifts or cards save for the ones he had just placed there and he wondered if maybe she just didn't have anyone else to call. "What happened?" he asked.

"Ah occupational hazard" she said waving at her battered face dismissively. "Some guys like to get rough, sometimes they take it a little too far, some just want to create a diversion so they can run off without paying."

She had a black eye on one side and it was so badly swollen she could hardly open it; there was a cut under the other eye and several cuts and bruises across the rest of her face and arms.

"Do they have wi-fi here?" she said nonchalantly rummaging around in her bag for her phone.

"What happened?" James said again. He had checked the police report, even though it wasn't his department, and it said that Amelia had been found slumped under the arch of a bridge by the river covered in blood. She had been taken to hospital and been treated her for minor cuts and bruises and they were keeping her in for observation after a suspected concussion. 'What had really happened to her,' he thought, 'Who had done this?' He felt his anger stir.

"I told you it was just an over enthusiastic client"

"The police report said you were found under a bridge and you were covered in blood"

"Slight exaggeration, ok he roughed me up a bit, it probably just looked worse than it was, who do I ask for the wi-fi code? Nurse!"

"Amelia you need to take this seriously. There is a serial killer, possibly two serial killers still at large in this area; you can't just pass this off as nothing. Did you get a good look at the man who did this to you?"

"What makes you so sure it was a man?" she said with a wry smile, "Besides I thought you were being a friend coming here to visit me in my sick bed but all you're doing is looking for more leads in your investigation."

James sighed, "I have come here as a friend but I also want to get the person who did this to you and there is a link between the attack on you and some of the other violent crimes that have taken place recently, besides you shouldn't have to put up with this as an occupational hazard."

"It's the life I chose" Amelia said still looking at her phone. James walked around to the end of the bed while she was still distracted to try and get a look at her chart to see if it provided any more information about what had happened to her. It seemed to be a lot of numbers and medical information, he looked to the top and spotted her name, it had her initials AD. He looked at the card above her bed it said A DeSalvo.

James walked slowly round to the other side of the bed "Is there anyone you want me to call?" he asked "Family?"

Amelia was typing something on her phone her eyes fixed on the screen she shook her head "Nah" she said without looking at him.

James stared back at the name above the bed "I just have to make a phone call, I'll step out in to the corridor for a second, I'll be back."

"Ok" Amelia said still preoccupied with her phone.

James stepped out in to the corridor away from the eyes of the nurses and pulled his phone from his pocket and pressed the call button "Evelyn" he said before waiting for her to speak "where was Millie Anderson's body found today?"

"Near the river" she said.

"Where exactly? How far from the bridge?"

"About half a mile"

"And he was stabbed? The attack was frenzied so whoever did this would be in a mess right?"

"Yes, they'd be covered in blood"

James paused and his breath quickened "And the guy you said was our killer was copying the Boston Strangler, what was his real name again?"

"DeSalvo, Alberto DeSalvo."

"I'm at Hoddlesworth General Hospital I need you to get back up here ASAP, I haven't got time to explain you'll just have to trust me."

"Ok but...."

He hung up the phone and marched back down the ward. The curtains were now pulled all the way around Amelia's bed, he pulled them back forcefully. The bed was empty.

Chapter 70

James walked across the car park as fast as he could his heart was racing, Evelyn was already stood outside the station. "What's going on?" she asked.

"I think I know who the other killer is." He walked past her and through the entrance doors, Evelyn ran after him.

"What? Who?" Evelyn asked.

"Amelia."

"What? That hooker?"

"Yes, it was what you said about there being a possibility the killer could be a woman."

"Yeh but I was joking. Women kill subtly, they poison their victims or they kill vulnerable people like children or the elderly. They don't display this level of violence."

"What about Rose West or Myra Hindley?"

"They committed their crimes alongside a man."

"Exactly."

Evelyn looked around and chewed her finger nails "So where is Amelia now?" she asked.

"I don't know" said James.

"What?"

"She was in a bed at the hospital when I called you and when I got back she was gone. She must have realised I was on to her."

They reached the incident room Oscar was sitting at what had now become his desk going through an evidence box.

"We need to go public, launch an appeal." Evelyn said.

Oscar looked up, "What's happened?" he asked.

"James has figured out who are other killer is"

"But she got away and now she's on the run. We can't launch an appeal, we'll cause mass panic" said James.

"There already is a mass panic and people already think we're not doing enough. If she kills again and it gets out we let her get away, we'll all be for the high jump."

"Evelyn's right" said Oscar, "We need the public on our side, get everybody out looking before someone else gets killed."

Chapter 71

"Thank you for coming" James said and he reached out and shook her hand, "its Mrs Taylor isn't it?"

"Yes, that's right, Helen Taylor, I'm Jane's, or Amelia's, Grandmother. When I saw her picture on the news I knew I had to get in touch."

"Mrs Taylor…"

"Oh Helen, please." He ushered her through the lobby of the police station and led her in to a small office and closed the door.

"Ok Helen, we believe your granddaughter may have been involved in a number of recent murders. She is currently on the run, is there anything you can tell us, anything at all, that might give us a clue as to her whereabouts?"

Helen fiddled with the cuffs on her dress. "is there any chance I could have a glass of water?" she asked.

"Of course," said James. He left the room and came back with a glass of water placing it on the table in front of Helen.

Helen took a sip from the glass; her hands were shaking as she lifted it and some on the contents dripped down on to the table. "I saw her picture on the news; I had been wondering with all these murders, it did cross my mind. I was ashamed of myself for even thinking it. She was such a lovely child, always playing with her brothers, keeping them in line, little miss bossy boots I called her. She was the mother hen of the family as soon as she could walk and talk, she had to be, I suppose. Her mother, well she struggled with four of them. I should have done more, I know I should but I had the farm to take care of. After my husband died it wasn't easy, there were staff but they were just doing a day's work, they didn't understand the responsibility I had. Tracey's drinking was getting worse though, she swore to me she calmed it down when she was pregnant but I'm not so sure. John left when Jane, or Amelia as you know her, was seven. He was weak, they were his children too. If Tracey's drinking was that bad he should have done more to protect them. I think he was just looking for a way out. We found out later he was with someone else pretty much straight away. I think he had her all along, I think Tracey knew about it as well that's why she kept drinking so much. She couldn't have been easy to live with I know, but to leave the children as well? Anyway, it was up to me to step in as usual, the children came to live with me on the farm, Tracey stayed where she was. John at least kept up with the mortgage repayments, I think he thought the children were still living there. I guess it made him feel better to think he hadn't abandoned them completely and if he didn't know they weren't there then that was his own fault for not visiting more often. I kept an eye on Tracey, I tried I really did. I offered to go to AA meetings with her, offered to try and get her into a detox programme but no she was on a mission to drink herself to death, and she succeeded. I had taken the children to visit her, Jane took the key off me and ran in first. She missed her mother the most I think, being the only girl. The boys were dawdling they were older too, I guess they had better memories about what their mother was like when she was drinking. It was Jane that found her, when I walked in she was just stood there staring. Tracey was slumped on the sofa still in her pyjamas a bottle of vodka at her side. There was vomit on her face down her front in her hair. They said that was what did it, she choked on her own vomit. I'm not sure how long she'd been there like that; I think it must have been a while. I blame myself, the house was a disgrace, filthy, no food in the cupboards, just vodka. I should have visited more, made her get help but she kept insisting she was fine. I shouldn't have taken the children round until I'd seen for myself. I made the boys go outside but Jane wouldn't leave, she wouldn't go near her mother she just kept staring at her. John didn't go to the funeral he said he wanted to leave the past where it was but he would send money for the children. Jane just lost interest in anything, the boys were a big help on the farm but Jane had no interest. When she was twelve I caught her in the barn, she had a chicken under her arm, at first, I thought she was cuddling it but when I got closer I could see that she was wringing it's neck. I was horrified, when I asked her what she was doing she said nothing and just stared at me blankly, the way she did at her mother that morning. Then she stood up, threw the dead chicken down and walked past me without a word. She was always in trouble at school, she tried to run away a few times but the police always brought her back. When she was sixteen she did it again. This time I didn't call the police. Well, she was sixteen so I didn't suppose they'd do much and to be honest I was glad she was gone. Everything was so much more peaceful when she wasn't there. Jane had too much of her mother in her, set on self-destruction. I did everything I could."

Helen took a tissue out of her bag and coughed into it nervously. "There is somewhere," she said looking at James "Somewhere I think she might have gone."

Chapter 72

"You sure this is the place?" James asked Helen.

"Yes" Helen said. "She used to come here whenever she ran away; she was normally in a pretty bad state when they found her, like mother like daughter I suppose."

James looked up at the overbearing church "Was she religious?"

"Ha, if she was it wasn't reflected in her behaviour, she used to come here with her mother, Tracey was quite religious, she was lapsed in many ways, but she did used to go to church every Sunday. I think she took comfort from it, hoping it would it would give her an answer she couldn't find in the bottom of a bottle. It didn't. Jane would go with her following her obligingly. I don't think Tracey even knew she was there half the time."

The wind whipped and a wind chime whistled in the distance. The air was thick. A storm was coming.

James leaned on the door handle Let's go" he said.

They walked up the path towards the door, Helen wrapped her scarf around her tightly, her face looked drawn. She waited for James to go around the car and lead the way up the path.

The door was heavy. The latch clicked, as James pushed the door, it resisted and creaked before eventually giving in and laboriously opening. They walked through carefully, only a faint glow from inside the church illuminated the lobby. There was silence. They both wanted to hear something, something that would tell them that they'd come to the right place. They waited, still silence.

"Jane!" Helen called out. Her breathing was heavy and fast. There was no answer.

"Amelia!" James called. Something shattered on the floor just in front of the main door, they walked towards it slowly, it was an empty bottle of vodka. James scanned the church but it seemed empty save for the two candles burning on the altar. The last remains of the sun burned through the stained-glass windows casting an orange pink glow across the room that slowly gave way to the imposing grey.

Helen followed James in to the church looking around frantically, "She's here. I know she is."

"And right you are granny" They looked up at the choir's balcony, Amelia leaned over, her hair bedraggled, she had made a vain attempt to apply makeup but the result was scarier than anything else. There was a cut on her hand and the blood was running down her arm.

"Jane! Get down from there!" Helen shouted.

Amelia sat down on the front bench and rested her feet on the balcony rail.

"Amelia" James said. She leaned forward and smiled.

"Yes?" she asked.

James didn't know what to say to her. He had played out this moment, catching the killer so many times in his head but he hadn't anticipated it would be like this, fragile delicate Amelia. Could she really have killed all those people?

"Amelia you need to come down, we need to talk to you" he said.

Amelia just threw her head back and laughed.

"I'm going up there "James ran out of the church and in to the lobby. He looked around and saw an open door almost concealed by the wood panelling. Behind it was a narrow stone stair way that led up to the balcony. James ran up it taking the steps two at a time. At one point he slipped and banged his knee on the edge of the cold stone. He cried out, but he pulled himself back up on to his feet and kept going until he came through a door at the top of the stairs and out to the balcony. Amelia stood up now, leaning with her back against the rail facing him. She put the vodka bottle to her lip and took another deep gulp.

"How did you meet Daniel Anderson?" James asked. He was out breath and sweating.

"Aw, jealous, are we?" she teased.

"You're Venus, aren't you?"

"One of my many aliases, I can be whoever I want to be depending on how I might feel that day."

"How did you meet him?!" James yelled and his voice echoed around the building.

"How do you think, he was my client."

James leaned on the edge of one the long benches "Why did you do it? How did he get you involved in this sick game?"

Amelia laughed again this time uncontrollably, hysterically. "How did Daniel get me involved? Oh my."

She looked away and continued laughing, pulling at the edges of the label on the vodka bottle.

James was getting angry now, this needed to end, he needed answers, "What's so funny?" he asked, his teeth on edge.

Amelia stopped laughing and looked at him smiling blissfully. "I think you'll find the shoe was very much on the other foot. Daniel was a client, at least I let him think that but I sought him out. I needed a bit of help, a bit of muscle. I'd managed to avoid any heavy lifting, leaving my tokens where they fell but I knew I was never going to win that way. My opponent clearly had more strength than me. I got Daniel to help with Craig. They thought it was a game at first. I handcuffed Craig to the bed and told Daniel to watch, they were excited, then I slit Craig's throat. I don't think either of thought it was real but it sunk in quick enough." She let out a little laugh "Daniel helped me move the body and he insisted on cleaning up afterwards even though I told him it wasn't necessary. Then he started freaking out. I had to make sure he kept quiet."

James could feel his heart rate quicken, the sweat pouring "Daniel was your opponent? Why would he help you?"

Amelia swayed the vodka bottle in front of her lips and giggled. Then it dawned on him, Daniel was another Wayne, a helper, the other killer was still out there.

"You killed his son to keep him quiet? But you've been advertising everything you've been doing on the internet for everyone to see why would you care about keeping him quiet?"

She shrugged, "Getting help was against the rules but as he went and confessed I guess I've lost now anyway."

Amelia's face snarled "You should have seen him after he dumped Craig's body; he was in bits, snivelling and crying, it was pathetic. He said he wanted out, I tried to explain it wasn't that simple when you're in the game, you're in the game until you win or lose, but he wouldn't listen so I had to make him understand." She took another gulp of vodka.

"You killed a child? Jane, how could you?" Helen was on the balcony at the top of the stairs breathless and shaking.

"It's Amelia! And yes, I did, so what? Kids are annoying, why should his life be deemed any more important than the other people I killed?"

"Who else did you kill Amelia?" James asked.

"Oh, you want to know which ones were mine. I did claim them all in my blog. , Lucy Maxwell, Maureen Connolly, Jenna Bishop, Elizabeth Robertson, my dear Craig, I made fools of them; I made fools of all of them, and of course there was little Jake." Amelia pulled her fur coat around her tightly and smiled.

"Why?" Helen asked, tears rolling down her cheeks.

"Why not? It was just a game. And it wasn't my idea to start playing again if it hadn't been for that article in the newspaper we would never have got back in touch."

"What article?" James asked.

"The one about the Worthington's 20th anniversary appeal."

"You killed the Worthington's? You must have only been a kid yourself?"

"Well yeh, that was the point, no-one was going to suspect a couple of kids. It was so easy too. We skipped school that day, we just walked right in there, and as soon as they saw the knives they did everything we said. We took the parent's first on the premise that if they did as they were told the kids would be alright, we were lying of course. We waited a little while until the parents were both pretty helpless but still able to see what was going on, then we did the kids too and put them to bed with mummy and daddy. Then we went down stairs and drank orange squash in the kitchen, and then we walked home."

Amelia drank her more vodka.

"Why the Worthington's, why that family?" said James

"Ask Carrie" Amelia answered.

"You are sick!" Helen seethed. Amelia just stared at her; she took another drink from the bottle of vodka, then hurled it at her grandmother. It hit her square on the head and she fell backwards, lost footing on the top step then tumbled back down the stair. She screamed as her head banged on every step, then there was silence.

James turned to run down the stairs to try and help her.

"Oh dear" Amelia said "it looks like granny's not going to get to see her wish come true" James turned as she stood on top of the rail on the edge of the balcony.

"Was Daniel your opponent? Amelia!" James screamed desperately but Amelia never answered she just leaned forward silently then fell and landed in a crumpled heap in the aisle of the church below.

Chapter 73

James kicked a stone in to the canal and watched it splash and sink beneath the surface. His gentle stroll ground to a halt; he put his hands in his pockets and stared across the water. He hadn't known her at all. How could she be capable of such things? He wiped away a small tear and continued to walk down the tow path.

He walked until he came to the turning then followed the path through the trees until it came to the clearing of the cemetery at the end. He walked down the rows of gravestones until he got to the spot he knew so well. He stood with his hands in his pockets and was still for a few moments.

"I should have brought you some flowers Rach." He said looking at the headstone in front of him, "Sorry. I guess I always was a bit rubbish at stuff like that. I wish I hadn't been, you know that don't you? I would do anything for the chance to make that up to you now." He knelt down, picked a blade of grass and began playing with it. It was quiet, peaceful, here. James liked to come here to think, to talk to Rachel, and sound her out about whatever was on his mind. He often found it helped.

He was lost in the quiet when suddenly he became aware of someone standing behind him, "I've seen you here before," a voice said. James stood up and turned around. Oscar was standing behind him, his coat zipped up, his hands in his pockets. "My wife's buried just over there," he nodded to the far corner of the cemetery, "I've seen you here a couple of times."

"Yeh I don't come as often as I should." James said.

"I'm sure there aren't any rules about that" said Oscar "I don't really think you need to come to places like this to remember the dead, you can remember them anywhere. It's the guilt that drags me, I didn't make enough effort to spend time with Marie when she was alive so I feel like I should at least try now. Not that it really makes a difference now, just eases my conscience a little."

"I like coming here" said James "helps me think."

"I heard, about Amelia."

James was quiet. "She killed the Worthington's. That was your case."

"It almost drove me to the brink that case."

"I asked her why, she said 'ask Carrie'"

Oscar looked at him. Carrie had disappeared; he knew she was hiding something.

"She didn't do it alone though" James continued "she kept saying 'we' 'we did it. And it's not Daniel, I think he was just used to help her, same as Wayne was. That means there's still one killer out there."

"Do you need a lift to the station?"

"That would be helpful, thanks. I walked down here, thought it might give me chance to think."

They turned and walked through the damp grass back towards the car park. "Have you got kids?" James asked.

"No" Oscar replied "Marie always wanted them but I always had something else I needed to achieve at work first."

"If you did though, you'd put photographs up of them at home, wouldn't you? You know holiday photos school pictures?"

"Erm, yeh I guess so, why?"

"Something's been bugging me. I visited Evelyn at home the night you suggested we all go to the pub; she hadn't been in work because she said her daughter, Lauren, was ill. Now I know she has a photograph of her on her desk but her house was bare, there wasn't one single photograph of her anywhere. Anyone who didn't know her wouldn't even think she had a kid."

They opened the doors and got in Oscar's car. Oscar began putting on his seatbelt "Well maybe she's moved, or been decorating recently and she hasn't got around to putting them up again?"

"I suppose it could be something like that." Oscar started the engine and they drove back to the police station.

Chapter 74

One year earlier

Gladys Findley was 93. She had five children 19 grandchildren and five great grandchildren. She had been a primary school teacher for 45 years. The matriarch of her family, the pillar of her community. Today she sat in her arm chair looking out of the window at the rain waiting for someone to come and put her to bed. It was 6:30 pm. They would be here soon. The front door opened. She didn't hear any talking though today. Must be just one of them. Budget cuts. They weren't supposed to send them on their own in case Gladys attacked them. Chance would be a fine thing Gladys thought. She couldn't even get to the toilet these days without the aid of a hoist and at least one other person. Maybe that's why they've given up sending two of them, she thought, can't even be counted at a threat anymore. .

Footstep climbed the stairs, the bedroom door opened. The carer said nothing; Gladys heard her rummaging around in her bag behind her. "You new?" Gladys asked. There was no reply. "Oh well I suppose I'm not worth talking to these days, silly old woman, on the scrap heap.

Gladys had become so engrossed in her bitterness she hadn't noticed the person had come and stood behind her, then she noticed the glow of the street lights reflecting on the blade.

Monday 14th October 2019

Shame you missed her. First move of the game, it took me ages to find her and then she wouldn't even let me finish. She was terrified though. That made me smile. Now time for the last move, oh sorry did you think this was over? I don't like to win like that I'll win in the place where your jealously caused you to lose your temper.

Chapter 75

It was early. The office was quiet save for the odd click of a mouse and the rumble of the cleaners hoover.

James clicked the kettle on and stood mesmerised as the steam rose out of the spout and the water rumbled and bubbled inside. The switch clicked and he went through the motions of making coffee, his mind still on the case and the dead ends he had come to. He picked up his coffee cup and wondered over to his desk.

"Morning" James jumped slightly he wasn't expecting anyone else to be in so early. Evelyn stood up and walked towards him "I have to get my own I take it?" she said with a smile.

"Sorry" James said "I didn't think anyone else would be here this early."

"It's ok. I've just finished my third for this morning so it's probably best I take it easy for a bit anyway." Evelyn carried her empty mug at to the kitchen at the back of the office and James heard her washing it.

"What time did you get here?" he shouted to her.

"Erm, I think it was about six"

"You have got the bug"

"I couldn't sleep. I just kept going over and over each case in my mind. I was sure I was missing something so I thought I might as well get up and come in to work and go over the files again."

"What about Lauren? "James asked

"What? Oh she was at her dads"

James took a sip of coffee as Evelyn walked back in carrying a glass of water "You two on good terms then?"

"Well kind of. You know for Lauren's sake. Anyway, I think I may have found something."

James put his mug down on the desk "What is it?"

"I think we have an earlier victim"

"What? When?"

"It's not recent, I was doing some digging and found this, Gladys Finley found dead in her nursing home a few months ago, the same day in fact as the 20th Anniversary of the Worthington murders. The post mortem said she died of natural causes but I was thinking about what you said about Amelia comparing herself to the Boston Strangler. He had a victim like that too Mary Mullen, she was thought to have died of natural causes, however when DeSalvo was arrested he confessed to breaking in to her house with the intent of killing her but she was so scared she had a heart attack and died and he just left. The police had no reason to suspect foul play was involved until he confessed."

"So why did he confess?"

"Because he wanted the credit."

"Amelia didn't confess to this."

"Exactly, that means it must have been her opponent"

"Ok so what does this mean?"

"Amelia killed Jake Anderson that was the last move, now it's her opponents turn."

"But she's dead, surely that means the other guys won?"

"I don't think it's that simple. This game is strategic, like chess, it's not about how many pieces you have taken but what pieces you take and winning is everything. Winning by default just wouldn't be good enough."

"Ok well keep looking. I want to know if there are any more clues about who the next victim is going to be, we can't let any more people die and we have to at least look as though we have some leads from somewhere."

"Yes Boss."

"Oh, and Evelyn…"

"Yes?"

"Well done."

"Thanks Boss"

Evelyn smiled and walked back to her desk.

*

"James!" Evelyn called. James looked up bleary eyed and forlorn, it was still only early afternoon but it felt like it had been a long day already. "I think I've got something" she said waving him towards her computer screen.

There was a new blog post showing on the screen "Look" she said pointing at the last line where 'Your jealously caused you to lose your temper. "I think I know where this is. I think it's the same car park where Jenna Bishop's body was found. Amelia cut her hair and wiped all her makeup off, she was jealous. Maybe we can intercept the killer before the next victim is murdered."

"Right let's go" James said grapping his jacket from the back of the chair.

"Wait" Oscar looked up from where he was working "How can you be sure this isn't a trap? If the point of this game is to take out victims with the highest value maybe killing a senior police officer could be the move that cinches victory. You've already been attacked once."

"That's a risk I'm prepared to take" James said.

"We need to check this out make sure we have back up in place."
Oscar stood firm with his hands in his pockets, James could almost feel
the stare of a disapproving father on him and his neck prickled.

"We need to act now or this killer could slip through our fingers
again and I'm not going to let that happen. Need I remind you that this is
my investigation and you're just a passenger."

"Is that right? Well it was a different story when you were begging
me for help. When you had no idea where to turn."

"You've served your purpose maybe it's time you left this to us
now old man."

Oscar stared and did not blink. His hands tightened in to fists
"Fine" he said "You two go" he continued staring. James pulled his jacket
on and looked away. Evelyn exchanged a look with Oscar then looked
away and left the room too.

Chapter 76

The smell wasn't the same anymore, not since the smoking ban, but those warm soggy beer mat smells still made him feel at home. It was quiet at this time of day, just the way he liked it. He looked around at the others there. Two women sat in a booth in the top corner both looking business like in smart stiff suits. One was making notes, the other held her hands folded in front of her and sat up very straight. Oscar guessed this was probably an interview, why here? He thought. Maybe the woman making notes ran the business from home and didn't want strangers there, or maybe she actually wasn't that important and didn't have an office in which to conduct an interview. The folded-hands woman kept adjusting her jacket, she looked uncomfortable like it had been a while since she's worn it and it was now a little snugger than she remembered. Maybe she was returning to work after maternity and wanted to get some independence back? The scuff marks on her shoes spoke more of necessity.

The thick heavy velvet curtains had been pulled back in fractions allowing rays of sunlight in to the grey room, the dust danced on them like a newly discovered life form.

There were two other men in the pub, both sitting alone. One of them was a balding, middle aged, overweight man, greying around the temples, tired of life. He sat slowly supping at a pint of bitter never taking his eyes from the racing pages of the newspaper in front of him. Looking for excitement, looking for a way out of his life? Oscar knew those feelings only too well.

The other man was younger, though his grey, tired, eyes betrayed his youth. He sat upright in his seat, tapping his fingers on his knee, checking his phone every few seconds and occasionally glancing at the door between frantic gulps of orange juice. Who was he waiting for? A date? A dealer?

Oscar sat on a stool at the corner of the bar. This had always been his favourite position, where he could survey the people, his people, the people who sought solace in drink.

"What can I get you mate?" the solitary barman asked as he finished wiping a beer glass with a tea towel.

"Scotch" Oscar said then paused "And make it a double please, no ice."

The barman returned moments later and placed the glass in front of Oscar on the bar. He handed over his money without listening to the price, his eyes transfixed on the gleaming orange gold liquid inside the glass. He closed his eyes and he could taste the bitter sweetness without it needing to touch his lips, feel the warmth as it slipped down his throat, the rush of adrenaline as the alcohol flittered through to his bloodstream and the calming sense of ease and numbness as it made its way to his brain. He opened his eyes and looked back down at the glass, he placed his fingers on the rim and swirled it around. The smell hit his nostrils and he closed his eyes again and sighed. He would wait. He pushed the glass slightly to one side, still within arm's reach and opened his briefcase and placed the files on the bar. He would go over them again one more time, and then he would have a drink.

It had never occurred to him that the killer could have been a woman. He had never heard of a woman committing such acts of violence, especially a woman as delicate as Amelia. She had help for at least one of her victims, they knew that, but most of them she killed alone. They had trusted her they didn't see her as a threat, but she was so angry maybe that had made up for her lack of physical strength?

The other killer though was different, more organised, methodical, stronger? Or were they? Wayne must have helped at some point so maybe the other killer wasn't that strong after all. He must have a slight build whoever he was. Oscar mentally corrected himself, he shouldn't keep assuming the killer was a 'he', that was old fashioned maybe James was right. He noticed Evelyn had never made that mistake.

It was starting to rain outside. The sky had darkened and the dust particles had died and gone. Oscar looked down at the notes he's been making then quickly packed the files away. He put on his coat and searched frantically for his car keys. He took another look at the whiskey picked up the glass and inhaled deeply. Then he placed it back on the bar untouched, and left.

Chapter 77

The rain was heavy. The drops hit the windscreen and splodge bigger each time merging into one another until the view was completely obscured. James sat staring forward, Evelyn by his side.

"How are we supposed to see anyone in this?" he tapped steering wheel in frustration "The killer could be right out there and we wouldn't even see him.

"The killer will be here" Evelyn said.

James shook his head "Nah I don't know about this. I think this could be another wild goose chase. What if he's lead us here to distract us from what he is really doing? Murdering another victim? What if Oscar was right?" he dropped his hands over his eyes. He was breathing heavily now.

Evelyn leaned over placing one hand on his shoulder "You are going to find your killer today" she whispered.

He looked up suddenly and met her eyes "I can't have another life on my conscience, on my record. I let this guy kill again and that's any hope of promotion gone and I'm not sure I can carry on sleeping at night if there are many more. I see their faces when I close my eyes. All those people, good people, and the people they left behind, all because I wasn't smart enough to stop some crazy game."

Evelyn stared right at him "You won't have any more souls on your conscience. You will find the second killer today. I promise."

Chapter 78

At the top of the slip road Oscar frantically turned his head from left to right trying to make out a gap in the traffic. The wipers were on the fastest speed but the rain still obscured his vision. He would just have to go for it. He pulled out onto the roundabout he heard the screech of breaks, the crunching of metal as his car was pushed up onto the verge. The driver's side door was squashed against the railing. He tried with every ounce of his strength to open the door but it was jammed. He undid his seat belt and climbed over the passenger side and opened the other door. His body ached all over, the rain still poured, the day was thick and grey and a lorry driver was swearing at him. He looked down the hill, he could see the car park and decided to make a limping run. The lorry driver was still swearing and it got louder as Oscar limped away "I have to go!" he said.

Chapter 79

James turned away from Evelyn and stared back out in to the rain. It was late the car park was empty, why would the killer choose this spot, who could the intended victim be? "I need to stay with it" he said. "Stay focused. It just felt like we were so close, I thought we had them."

"Amelia was unstable, opportunistic. In chess, half the battle is not just planning your own moves but also predicting what moves your opponent will make."

"So why give us this clue then?"

"Maybe you were right, maybe they want to brag. Let you know how clever they are."

In the distance James thought he could see the shape of a man limping towards them. He opened his mouth to ask Evelyn if she saw it too when he felt something cold and round pressed against his temple. He turned to look at Evelyn. Her dark brown eyes looked into his. They did not blink, they did not flicker. She had kept her promise.

"Check mate" she said.

Chapter 80

James couldn't move. He just stared in to her dark hard eyes "You?" he said.

Evelyn stayed silent.

"It was you?" James said again. The fear he felt at having a gun pointing to his head soon subsided to anger. She had been by his side all this time, had she been leading him astray? Deliberately sabotaging the investigation? "Why?" he asked.

She laughed, "Well that's the thing everyone wants to know isn't it? Why? No matter how gruesome, how unjust, everyone wants to know why. But why does there always have to be an explanation? Maybe we just did it for the hell of it; maybe we did it because we could."

"Did you kill the Worthington's? Did you and Amelia wipe out that family?"

She smiled "Yes. Yes, we did."

"You killed three children and their parents. You left Carrie Worthington with no family she was fifteen and she had no-one." He was shouting now, Evelyn pushed the gun harder against his temple and he quietened down.

Evelyn shrugged "Carrie knew what she was getting herself in to."

"What? Are you saying she was in on the murder of her whole family?"

Evelyn laughed "She wasn't just in on it, she caused it."

"How?"

"Well you'll have to ask her that."

"That's what Amelia said, I'm asking you."

"Seeing as you're the one with a gun pointing at your head I don't think you're really in a position to be issuing demands, *sir*."

"Innocent people have died, died for the sake of your sick game. You're a mother"

Evelyn carried on staring at him but laughed hysterically "You believed that? Come on you figured it out at soon as you came around to my house, I didn't have any kids, I got that picture on my desk from the internet. Just all part of the game."

"Why would you pretend to have a child?"

"Amelia modelled herself on The Boston Strangler, me? I was Ted Bundy. Normal, respectable, like so many other people you might know. So, I thought I'd invent a child for myself make me seem even more normal and respectable"

"You said Ted Bundy was a sex attacker?"

"Yes, and I did try to tell you that these killings weren't copycats. We didn't want to mimic them, copy their crimes; we admired their fame, their notoriety, the fact they got away with it for so long. Jane, or Amelia, she had a thing for humiliating people making fools of them, I guessed she'd been humiliated herself a fair few times and wanted to get her own back. Me, I just like to surprise people." She smiled.

"That day Tom Hodden was killed. That was you in the house."

"Well done. It was also the day I killed Wayne, he just couldn't resist blabbing. I told him Oscar had figured us out. He must have followed him from the station; he was too much of glory hunter, in it for the winning rather than the thrill of the game. You almost caught me, then I started preparing the cellar for next victim, the kind-hearted charity worker who jogged in the park every day, big and strong, he was worth a lot. Then you two idiots got in the way so I had to change my plan. I asked him for help fixing a flat tyre, when he bent down to look at it I hit him on the head with the jack and left him where he was. I had other things in mind but with my assistant no longer of any use and nowhere to take the body, I had no choice.

"Then you just waited for the call and took charge of a murder scene like it was a normal day at the office."

Evelyn smiled; she obviously saw this remark as compliment.

"I did have some issues with my car though, I wasn't lying about that. I had to get a replacement I couldn't risk you recognising the old one."

"You tried to run me off the road?"

"You were getting too close. That was why I sent that message the following morning. I was hoping there wouldn't be a reply but I guess you eluded me. It won't happen again. All life is a game. Sometimes you have to take out a few pawns to come out on top, but Oscar was right, you should listen to him more, killing a police officer that would be a good move. That would make me the winner." She looked at him and smiled.

Chapter 81

Oscar struggled across the car park, his leg hurt, he had done some damage to his knee but he had to keep going. The rain was coming down in buckets now, he could barely see anything in front of him. Maybe they weren't even here; maybe she had lead him off somewhere else? He looked up and saw James' car in the distance, if could get to him he could warn him, he tried to walk faster and faster through the rain. He heard a gunshot.

Chapter 82

The rear windscreen shattered. James opened his eyes slowly, he lifted his head, it hurt. Evelyn was slumped forward in the seat next to him, blood was running down on to the floor beside her; he turned to look through the rear smashed windscreen. Through the gap he saw a battered old Fiesta driving away. He got out and to run after it, his ears were ringing and his head throbbed, the car had gone. All he saw of the driver was a flash of blonde hair. He ran back to the car to check on Evelyn, when he got there, the car was empty.

Chapter 83

SOCO were examining the car. It had stopped raining and heavy clouds had lifted to leave a few wispy traces. The sun was setting behind them and turned the sky pink and orange. Oscar stood in the car park being treated by paramedics. James walked over to him.

"What's the verdict?" James asked

"Well I'll live but I think my premiership days are over" Oscar joked.

James smiled, looked up and scanned the horizon.

"She can't have got far" Oscar said "The bullet must have hit her, she would have been wounded."

"I wouldn't put anything past her" said James.

The SOCO walked over with a plastic bag containing a small piece of metal. "We recovered the bullet from the car" he said "Must have gone straight through."

"Could it have been a fatal injury?" James asked.

"Hard to saying without knowing exactly where it hit" said the SOCO, he looked at James, "There was a lot of blood though."

James nodded. He understood.

"Can you tell what kind of gun it was fired from?" Oscar asked.

"We can't be sure at this stage but it looks like it came from a rifle or shotgun, the kind you use to kill rabbits or pheasants."

"The kind you might keep on a farm?" asked Oscar.

"Yeh, something like that." The SOCO walked away with his bag.

James sighed "Chances are she's bleeding to death in an alleyway somewhere."

"Maybe" said Oscar.

"Anyway, what are you worried about you'll be retired soon, crown green bowling and bridge club for you. DIY, gardening, daytime TV, I bet you can't wait."

Oscar smiled "we'll see." He said.

Friday 18th October 2019

You pass so many people every day but do you really see them; people on the bus, in the supermarket, at a football match. How many of them could be a serial killer? No label on their head, no evil sneer. Perfectly ordinary. A serial killer could be a perfectly ordinary person, handing over your change at the supermarket, delivering your post or sitting next to you on the bus. Right now.